HER FIERCE SEAL

MIDNIGHT DELTA SERIES, BOOK 6

CAITLYN O'LEARY

PASSIONATELY KIND PUBLISHING INC.

To Those Who Have Served and Those Who Have Struggled

SYNOPSIS

Navy SEAL, Finn Crandall, still reeling from his last mission, is desperate for a purpose to bring him the redemption he needs.

Landing in Austin Texas, he meets the feisty Angie Donatelli. She's a private investigator on a quest to reunite a young girl with her stolen baby. Angie is tough and doesn't want or think that she needs help. When she's confronted with a man who won't take no for an answer, sparks fly and flames ignite. Angie finds herself falling for the sexiest and most stubborn man she has ever met.

When Finn and Angie team up to search for the missing baby, Finn's fierce protective instincts kick into high gear. As they dig deeper into the baby's disappearance, Finn's old nightmares get tangled up with the new horrors they encounter. Will Angie's unconditional love and Finn's inner strength be enough to fight the demons of his past and conquer the evils they're confronting today?

This book is a stand-alone but is best read as part of the series.

1

"FINN, GET LITTLE LIU AND HIS SICK FUCKING UNCLE BEFORE they get away!" Drake yelled.

Finn grinned ferally and grabbed a man with a gun, he shoved his arm up, and the bullet shattered a sconce high up on a wall. Finn slammed the man's arm down on his knee and listened for the satisfying crunch of bone and the man's howl of pain. Leaving him in a heap, he hurdled over him toward the two men who had been at the center of the unfolding carnage.

One of the men Finn despised was dead on the ground and the other that he hated grinned at his arrival.

"You're here," he shouted in greeting. The stupid asshole didn't realize Finn was his executioner. Finn looked at the man he had pretended to like when he had infiltrated the human trafficking ring. "Do you believe this shit?" Howard grinned. He was clearly enjoying the death and destruction surrounding them.

Howard pointed his gun towards something behind Finn and within seconds a blossom of red spread over his chest.

"Got him, Finn!" Drake yelled from across the room.

"Goddamit, Drake. He was mine!" Finn yelled to his fellow Navy SEAL.

Then Finn turned to Liu and Jiang, who stared at him in panic as they realized he was not on their side. Finn loved watching the two men's dawning realization that this was the end of the line.

Just forty-eight hours ago he had seen Liu's underlings torture a young girl and had been helpless to do anything about it. They'd also threatened and assaulted a woman he liked and admired. The younger Liu was responsible for buying and selling young women around the world. Pictures swirled inside Finn's head. Rage swelled within him, and he knew he would not let either of them see the inside of a prison cell. They needed to die and die painfully.

Albert Liu proved he was as stupid as he was evil when he tried to run past Finn. He held out his foot and tripped him, then watched dispassionately as the man's head hit the floor with a loud crack. Jiang Liu huddled on the floor near the armoire covered with broken vases and strewn flowers and stared up at Finn, his terror palpable.

Finn hauled up Little Liu and threw him on the counter, uncaring if he was cut by the shattered glass. He pulled out his gun and smiled at the man's horror.

"Don't kill me," he begged through bloody lips.

"Too late. You signed your death warrant years ago. Now I'm just deciding how badly you're going to die." Finn slowly slid his gun down the side of the man's jaw, and Jiang whimpered at his feet. He slammed his boot on Jiang's hand and twisted. His howl of agony helped relieve some of Finn's own pain and rage.

"Now where were we, Albert?" he asked the man lying in front of him. He caressed his face with the gun, as it stroked downwards it smeared blood down his neck, and he enjoyed seeing the bright crimson against the blue steel of gunmetal. He continued to move the pistol lower until it was nestled against the man's crotch, then he shoved upwards. Hard. Liu grunted in pain.

"I'll do anything. I'm a rich man. Ten million dollars. Cash. It's yours."

"Not enough," Finn growled.

"A hundred million in diamonds," Liu promised. "It'll take me a few days."

Finn shoved the gun harder against the man's testicles. "You piece of shit. You don't get it. Do you?"

"What? Tell me. I'll give you anything. Say anything." The man practically bled terror.

"Let's start with I'm sorry." Finn saw the confusion in Liu's eyes and stared at the dumb fucker in disbelief.

"You mindless fuck." Finn's head was going to explode.

"I'm sorry. I'm sorry."

The words were distorted. As if coming through a long tunnel

"Of course, I'm sorry."

It was too little, too late. Finn's finger tightened.

"Finn!" Darius Stanton yelled. Finn released the pressure on the trigger, as his surroundings came into focus and he saw the bullets still flying around the room. Funny, he hadn't noticed it before. As a SEAL he usually noticed things like that. He shook his head again to clear it.

He turned to his friend and fellow teammate.

"Hey, Dare." He attempted a smile.

"Whatchya doing?" Darius asked.

Finn looked at Dare, then at Little Liu, who was lying on the counter, and the Sick Old Fuck, who lay on the floor bleeding beneath his boot. He looked back at his friend and smiled. "I've decided to shoot his dick off and watch him bleed out. Then I'm going to do the same thing to this one." He pressed his foot deeper and harder onto the old man's hand. He felt the bones crush. Satisfying.

"You can't do that, partner," Darius said. Finn saw he was serious. Odd. Finn would have thought Dare would have understood how necessary this was.

Then he realized Dare hadn't been at the farmhouse. He hadn't talked to those girls. He didn't know everything. Fuck, he didn't even know what they had done to Dare's woman.

"Do you know how many bruises Rylie has because of them?" His friend jerked his head and glared at Liu lying on the armoire, his face a mask of rage.

"Dare, I know about the baby farm. Liu's the cause of this mess. Look around. People died tonight. Did you know women were thrown overboard off of a cargo ship? He needs to die. He needs to die badly."

Finn watched his friend and fellow teammate closely and began to relax. He noted the fighting behind him began to die down. The good guys were winning. Then his eyes widened as Rylie ran up behind Dare. *Fuck!* He had left her upstairs in a safe place. She wasn't supposed to be down here where it was dangerous!

"Finn, you can't do this!" Rylie entreated with pleading eyes. Finn was scared to death. Things might have quieted down, but the area wasn't totally secure.

"Dammit, Rylie! I told you to stay upstairs where it was safe," he yelled. She didn't back down, her long blonde hair flew around her, and she looked like a Valkyrie.

"Well you shouldn't have decided to commit murder," she said as she pointed to the worthless piece of shit trembling under his gun.

"It's not murder. I'm taking out the garbage. I'm saving the state some money. Call it what you will, it's not murder." He huffed out a laugh. She was cute. She was perfect for Dare.

"Isn't it enough you already killed Mike and Howard?" She gestured to the two men on the floor. He took a moment to glance at the two corpses beside Jiang, hating them. Howard would have raped a young girl if he hadn't ripped him off her, and Mike had stood by, ready to take his turn.

"I didn't have the pleasure. However, I can kill these two."

Rylie turned to Darius.

"You have to stop him," she begged her lover.

"I don't," Darius said.

"He'll go to prison," she argued. Finn knew he was about to execute these two in cold blood, but it was the right thing to do. Why couldn't Rylie see it that way?

"Nah, it'll be an unfortunate accident during a shootout. Two accidents, when he gets done with the sick old fuck of an uncle." Darius pointed to Jiang, who was sobbing beneath Finn's boot.

"Please, Finn, I care about you. I don't want you to feel bad about this for the rest of your life."

Pottery shattered next to Albert Liu's head, spraying water and lilies all over him. A large Asian man advanced and Dare easily shot and killed him, while Jiang screamed and pushed at Finn.

The gun went off. Blood and gore covered his hand as Albert's body blew apart beneath the muzzle of his gun. Albert Liu's shrill screams painted the air. Finn smiled with satisfaction. Justice at fucking last. His stomach unclenched just a little. But it wasn't over. Jiang Liu was about to die of stupidity, and he'd watch with pleasure.

The older man crawled across the floor towards the gun the dead man had dropped.

"Jiang, don't make me kill you," Darius called out. Jiang grabbed for it anyway. Darius shook his head in disgust and shot the sick old fuck in the head.

Finn felt the blood begin to cool on his hand, and wiped it off on his pants. He glanced at Albert's face, just to make sure the asshole was dead.

Still, none of this was enough to make up for all of the horrors that had gone on. There had been too many innocents. Just too many damned innocents.

It had been five weeks since the bloody shootout in British Columbia, Canada. And Finn was sitting in his lieutenant's living room surrounded by his Navy SEAL teammates and their women. They had been up all night brainstorming how they could help the girls they'd rescued. Yes, there were government agencies involved, and some of the girls had been reunited with their families, but some had slipped through the cracks, and those were the ones they were focusing on.

There were very few people on this Earth that impressed Finn as much as these people did. They were the best.

"Dammit, Clint, listen to me, and quit waiting for Sophia's next batch of cookies," Lydia growled at her man. "Ophelia is with her family, it's Ursula I'm worried about."

Clint sighed and ran his hands through his hair, then placed them back on his computer keyboard.

"Lydia, cut him some slack," Rylie admonished. "There are so many different names, everybody is bound to get confused. I should have made up a name chart or something."

"He's not paying attention, and if we don't do something quick," her voice trailed off and much to everyone's horror her face crumpled. Clint acted fast and pulled Lydia into his arms. He whispered into his fiancée's ear, and she curled up against him as her tears started.

"Damn," Drake breathed out. Finn knew what the big guy meant, no one expected hell-on-wheels Lydia to breakdown. Of course, after the torture she had endured at the hands of the cartel, she would always be a little more fragile than she appeared.

Fuck, if only they had gotten to that cabin an hour earlier.

"It's because of the babies," Beth Hidalgo, Lydia's sister said, interrupting his reverie. She had just walked in on the spectacle when she and Sophia brought out cookies. "Lydia is really torn up over the missing babies, she and Sophia have taken it the hardest."

Mason, the Midnight Delta lieutenant, held out his hand for his wife, and Sophia went and sat on his lap. Beth sat next to her fiancé, Jack Preston, another member of the SEAL team.

Again, Finn perused everyone in the living room. He wished everything would have just remained the same. That he could get back to the time before the mission when everything had been so joyful at this house, and he had been capable of smiling. Four contented couples, so much love. Less than four months ago he had been grinning from ear-to-ear when he had been a groomsman in Mason's wedding. Now everything was just another shade of gray.

For a time, everyone stayed quiet, lost in thought as they gave Lydia time to compose herself.

"I'm sorry I lost it," Lydia said finally as she looked up from Clint's arms.

"No need to apologize," Mason responded. "We're all on edge. We want to do what we can to assist the girls who were trafficked find new homes or reunite them with their families. And we sure as fuck want to hunt down those stolen babies and get them back into the arms of their mothers. It's just taking longer than we thought it would."

"Fucking bureaucrats," Drake's loud voice carried through the room. "I still can't believe how many of those motherfuckers have their thumbs up their asses trying to figure out whose job it is to help those girls because it's an international case. I know this crossed multiple borders, and only two of the girls were US citizens, but more should be done for them. I'm about ready to crack some fucking skulls!"

"Down Drake, you're not helping anything," Mason said tiredly. Sophia stroked the side of his face and Finn saw him take comfort in the small caress.

"We know this operation inside and out. No one can put the pieces together better than we can. So even if they did decide to help, they'd fuck things up," Rylie said with disgust. She turned to Lydia. "I know you're worried about Ursula, but Sophia has already got a couple of ideas about where she could stay."

"You do?" Lydia sat straight up on Clint's lap and stared at Sophia, who blushed.

"I didn't want to say anything until I was sure they wouldn't fall through. But yes, I know one family in particular that would love to have her come and stay with them. They're in San Bernardino. They're suffering from empty nest syndrome, and the idea of having Ursula stay for a year or two, until she gets on her feet, tickles them to death."

"They know she's pregnant, right?" Rylie asked.

"Yep. I told them everything. One of their daughters is currently serving in the Navy. That's how I knew to reach out to them," Sophia explained. "Beth and I went over and met with them yesterday. When we left, they were talking about buying Rosetta Stone for Ukrainian."

"Oh my God, that's another one taken care of," Rylie said, her eyes shining. "We can do this. We only have three more girls to place and five more babies to find. This will be a piece of cake."

"I love your positive attitude, sunshine." Drake's eyes lit up as he looked at Darius' fiancée. "Are you sure you want to hook up with Dare? I think you would be better off with me."

"Fuck off, Avery," Darius said to Drake. "Rylie is mine."

"Damn right I am. I have the ring to prove it." She smirked, holding out her left hand.

"Now, if he can only keep you out of trouble." Drake sighed.

"Are you kidding? I intend to live a boring life from this day forward. At least, after we find places for all of the girls and reunite all of the babies with their moms."

"Did you just say boring?" Drake asked Rylie. "I've met your brothers and sister. You're not going to be doing boring for the next forty years. I know everybody thinks that Georgie is hell on wheels, but trust me, it's going to be quiet little Charlie who's going to be the hell raiser."

Rylie looked at Drake in confusion.

"He's talking about Charlotte, baby," Dare explained to Rylie.

"You don't know what you're talking about Drake," Rylie sputtered. "Char is a good girl."

"She's going to find the right boy, and they'll be no stopping her." Rylie got up out of her seat and took a step towards Drake, and Dare grabbed her hand.

"He's baiting you. Don't listen to him. Stop it, Drake," he admonished his friend.

"Sorry Rylie. I was kidding, Charlotte is an absolute doll. Actually, I would love to see her kick up her heels."

"Yeah, me too," Rylie admitted.

"Hey," Clint said looking down at his computer. "We just got another hit. Seems like one of the web spiders we put out on the net picked up another couple who mysteriously adopted a child five weeks ago."

"Hot damn!" Lydia peered at Clint's computer screen.

Finn sat back a little further on the couch, listening to the team talk about the next steps. He wished he could feel even a tenth of what they were feeling, but he couldn't. He knew he wasn't the same man he was before the mission, and he never would be again. How do you ever come back after you've become a monster?

THE PACIFICO WENT DOWN SMOOTHLY. It was his second. He was in his favorite seat, at his favorite table, in his favorite bar overlooking the Pacific Ocean in San Diego. Soon the sun would set, and he was finally beginning to relax. He was doing the right thing.

The day after the all-nighter at Mason's house, Finn had finally come clean to the Midnight Delta Team about what had happened. Drake and Dare knew some fugly shit had gone down when he had been undercover at the farmhouse, but they'd had no earthly idea how bad it'd been. Normally, his confession would be something he would just tell his commander, but they all needed to know the kind of man he'd become. So he told them all as a group. He'd told them every ugly fucking detail. Even the stuff he'd held back when he'd initially talked to Drake up in Canada.

Even now, sitting in a spot that was basically paradise, chills raced down his spine. He started to gag as he set down his beer.

He thought back to the little bit of time he had worked undercover guarding the young women who had been trafficked. His mission had been to pretend to be one of the bad guys and keep them holed up in the farmhouse for two days until the auction. It had gone against every bone in his body not to break them out and take them to safety.

Yeah, but you didn't. Did you, Crandall?

Instead, he had acted like a sadistic asshole as they cried and begged to be released. One girl, who couldn't have been more than sixteen, had gotten down on her knees in front of him. She had pleaded in broken English to do anything to be allowed a chance to escape. Her meaning had been clear.

Another girl, who had been caught trying to run away, had been pulled back to the farmhouse by her hair and almost raped by two men before Finn had been alerted and stepped in. Suspicious of him, Mike and Howard had made Finn hold Penelope down while Howard forced her to drink a bottle of hot sauce as punishment. Part of his soul died that night.

Fast forward two days to the night of the auction and the shootout. He had to admit, Rylie and Darius had planned the takedown slicker than snot. The only discordant notes were that he hadn't been able to beat Howard and Mike to death the way they deserved. Still, he had killed Albert Liu, the man who had orchestrated the hell at the farmhouse. He only wished he could have prolonged his death. Thinking of the operation, of the defenseless women, cracked him wide open with helplessness and anger. Even now, a cloud of self-loathing threatened to swallow him whole.

Even almost two months after the events, he wasn't able to hide his rage as he would have liked.

He clenched and unclenched his fists. A new habit he had picked up. He closed his eyes and focused on the present. His buddies had invited him for a drink tonight. He looked at his watch. Any minute they'd arrive at the bar. It was just going to be a different bar than the one Finn was at. He knew they were planning an intervention. Finn tipped back his chair and closed his eyes, and played out what they would say.

Mason would start, God love the man.

"Finn, where have you been hiding? Haven't seen your ass around except at the base since you dropped your bomb. We told you it didn't matter. You did exactly what every one of us would have done in your shoes."

"Would you believe I started dating this girl?" Finn would start out.

"Fuck no! You're ducking us, and this shit has to stop." Drake would roar. *"Pull your guilt-ridden head out of your ass and talk to us."*

"What the big guy means is that we're here for you." A typical Dare comment.

"I know you are. I just don't feel like socializing. I want to focus on work."

Mason would look uncomfortable. He just knew it, because that's the kind of leader he was. The very reason for this intervention was because Mason was trying to arrange a safety net for Finn in his time of need. If that didn't work, Mason would sit him down privately and discuss the need to place him sick in quarters and counseling so he could work through his issues. Finn's chest tightened because he knew this man, and he would be with him every step of the way. God, there would never be anyone else he would want to serve under.

His phone rang, interrupting his musings. It was Drake.

"You fucker. Where are you?"

"Not there."

"Get your ass over here."

"I'm in Carlsbad," Finn lied. It was nice hearing Drake's frustration.

"Fucker." He heard him tell the others.

"Hey, Finn." It was Mason. Finn let out a sigh.

"Hi, Mase. Look, I'm sorry."

"I'm going to need to talk to you tomorrow. Can we meet in the morning in my office?" Mason's voice was soothing. Finn really liked this man, just hearing how he was attempting to help him made him respect him more. But Finn knew he was undeserving of his help.

"There's a letter on your desk requesting discharge." This time, Mason sighed.

"I'm not accepting it."

"You don't have a choice."

"I do." There was a long silence. Finn wasn't surprised to hear Clint's voice.

"Your letter will now be a request for leave, which our beloved leader will approve."

"You're going to forge my signature?" Finn was surprised that he was surprised. He should have known Clint would be willing to do something like that.

"Bet your ass I'm going to forge your signature." Mason got back on the phone.

"Now that I've accepted your request for leave, I want

you over at the house tomorrow night for dinner. Sophia misses you, and so does Billy. Apparently, the guy you've arranged as the substitute coach for the Lacrosse team sucks. That's an exact quote from Billy." Finn closed his eyes and pictured Mason's wife, Sophia, and her fifteen-year-old brother, Billy. He was going to miss them. Especially Billy, the kid was special.

"No can do boss. Please invite Mom and Rebecca instead. I have plans. I'm going off the grid for a while." Finn was about to disconnect the phone when Mason stopped him.

"Hold up, Crandall. You know we'll have your mom's six, right?"

Finn tightened the hold on his iPhone.

"I never doubted it for an instant. I've got to do this, Mase. I'll be back when I'm back."

Finn disconnected the call and removed the sim card. Mason would respect his privacy and give him the space he needed to get his shit together, but he wouldn't put it past Clint and Lydia to try to track his whereabouts through his phone. He was serious, he needed away. If they wanted to find him, he'd make them work for it.

He picked up the other phone his friend Declan had overnighted to him. He punched in the first name on the speed dial. He got voicemail.

"Declan. It's me, Finn. Give me a call. I'm a free agent for the time being. I'm working on something and could use some intel."

2

HE PULLED UP TO HIS MOTHER'S DUPLEX. HE'D THOUGHT about seeing her before the 'bait-n-switch' meeting with his teammates but knew they would respect his privacy...for a while. He took a deep breath and headed for the door.

"Finnius? Are you even listening to me?"

Finn looked up from the kitchen table and saw his mother was hovering over him. The last time he had seen her she had been at the counter chopping vegetables.

"You've been sitting at my table for over an hour with such a long face that the bread won't be able to rise." His mom put a plate of Norwegian butter cookies and a glass of milk in front of him.

"You must be worried," he said indicating the treats.

"I am." She sat across from him. She actually patted the pocket of her sweater and laughed. He came close to smiling. If his mom reached for a cigarette, she was stressed. She hadn't smoked in over fifteen years.

"Finn, honey, two years ago you had to pick me up off the floor when your granddad's Alzheimer's knocked me on my ass. All the while you were hurting as badly as I was. But you did what you always did, you cared for me, coaxed me into moving out here to be near you and make a new life. Hell, you dragged us both into counseling. You were a Godsend. But I know you have one of the most stressful jobs in the world."

"Are you kidding me, Mom? This is the job I wanted more than anything. I worked my ass off to become a SEAL. It was my dream."

"I'm not denying that, Finn. But you're not going to tell me that some of the things you do aren't life and death." His mother pushed the plate of cookies closer to him.

"Of course, they are." Finn grabbed a cookie, took a bite and a long drink of milk.

"When you came back two months ago, you weren't you. You've shut down." She got the carton of milk from the fridge to refill his glass, giving them both time to contemplate her words.

"Can you tell me about it?" she asked as she poured more milk into his glass.

"I can't." The two words came out harsh and ugly.

"Can you tell me how you feel?" she asked gently.

He sighed. "The cookies help."

She gave him a 'mom' look.

"They do. They make me feel like a kid again when a cookie could solve all my problems." He blew out a long breath. "Mom, things are pretty confused right now. I fucked up. I hurt some people."

She didn't immediately respond, and it was one of the things that made Evie Crandall so special. Yeah, she was totally on his side, but she was a thinker like him. She contemplated her responses, so he knew when the chips were *really* down, she wasn't just blowing smoke up his ass. At the same time, she'd have his back as fiercely as his team.

"Three questions."

"Shoot."

"Did they deserve to be hurt."

"Some did."

"The ones that did, did you hurt them on purpose?"

"Fuck yeah." He picked up another cookie and bit into it with relish.

"Well, then that's probably a good thing." She smiled. "The ones that didn't deserve to be hurt, did you hurt them on purpose?"

He didn't answer. But that was as good as answering, wasn't it?

"Oh, honey."

"Would you do it again, Finn?" she finally asked.

"God help me, Mom. Yes, I would. I had to do it to ultimately help them." His voice cracked, and he thought he'd throw up. He pushed away from the table. He had to get the fuck out of there.

"Wait, baby boy, what does Mason say? Does he say you crossed a line?" She looked up at him as he trembled, every one of his instincts said to run, but he hadn't said goodbye so he couldn't leave.

"He says he would have done the exact same thing. I don't believe him. He would have found a different way to handle it. I don't know how, but he would have. Any of the others would have. So Mason saying I made the right choice doesn't matter."

"No, it wouldn't." She sighed. She went around the table and grabbed him in a hard hug. He rested his head on her shoulder for a long moment before he pushed away.

Taking a step back, he cupped her cheek. "I've got to leave for a while."

Evie bit her lip.

"How long is a while?"

"I don't know." And he really didn't.

"Can you tell me where you're going?"

"I'm not sure yet. Even if I did know, I wouldn't tell you. The team is going to be dropping by, and they'll be asking questions. I don't want to put you in the situation where you have to keep things from them or lie."

"Will you check in?"

"Eventually." It pained him to see her pat her sweater pocket again, looking for an imaginary cigarette.

"You're hurting her!" Rebecca ran into the kitchen. "You need to tell her where you're going at least!" Finn stared in shock at the fifteen-year-old girl with her long brown hair swinging and her eyes blazing with anger.

"Rebecca, calm down, he doesn't mean to hurt me."

"It doesn't matter, Evie. He is." She turned back to Finn. "Don't be selfish. You need to promise to call her."

Finn was amazed that this girl, who had once been so quiet, was yelling at him and defending his mother. He was proud of the work his mother had done with her.

"You're absolutely right, Rebecca. I'm sorry. I promise to call her every two weeks, no matter what. Will that work?"

Her jaw jutted out. "Once a week."

The corner of his mouth lifted. "All right, once a week. Will that work?" Rebecca gave a short nod, then he saw her eyes fill with tears.

"Hey, hey, what's this about?" He stepped closer to her.

"I don't want you to go, Finn. I like having a big brother to talk to." He looked at the young girl, and his heart twisted. Suddenly, the girl who had been on her knees in the farmhouse was superimposed on top of Rebecca. He broke into a cold sweat and gritted his teeth. He knew logically he was still in his mom's kitchen and not back in time.

"I don't want you to go." Rebecca's voice.

"I'll do anything, please let me go." It was the other girl's voice.

Instead of brown hair and brown eyes, he saw blonde hair and blue eyes.

"Mom?" Finn called out.

"Finn?" His mom's voice helped to steady him. He blinked and was once again able to see Rebecca. He tried hard to give her the best smile he could, but it was pathetic, and he knew it. She looked up at him, confused, but then he held out his arms, and she hit him like a freight train.

"I love you, Finn." Her love floored him.

"I love having a little sister. You are one of the best things that has ever happened to me. I'll make sure to talk to *both* of my best girls every week."

"You better." His mom came over and wrapped her arms around them. He took comfort in it.

WHEN HE GOT into his car, there was a message on the burner phone.

Head to Austin, there is a project that needs your expertise.

He tried calling Declan again and got his voicemail. *Figures.* His childhood friend was probably ducking his calls at this point. What an asshole, he thought fondly.

He looked out the rearview window into the back of his El Camino at the pitiful amount of stuff that he had packed. He'd thought about putting his stuff in storage and getting out of the lease on his condo, but it seemed like too much of a bother. What's more, part of him really hoped he would be coming back to San Diego if he could ever get his shit together.

He stopped at a gas station near the highway and gassed up the car and stocked up on water before heading east. For the next four hours, he focused on traffic, until he got out of the more populated areas and hit desert. Then his brain began to consider what Declan's cryptic message might mean.

He and Dec had been friends since grade school. Both of their dads had worked together in Minnesota. Now Declan was one of the founding members of a group called the Shadow Alliance.

Declan had his fingers in pies all over the world. Finn regularly tapped Dec's organization when he needed something for the Midnight Delta team. It paid off having a network of far-flung friends. Even though he hadn't helped in the sex trafficking mission, Finn figured he had kept tabs on it. When the man said he had a project that needed Finn's expertise, he really hoped it was related to the missing babies. Midnight Delta didn't have the time or the resources to keep looking, and the longer the infants stayed missing, the more likely they would never be found.

His fingers got sweaty on the wheel of the car. His teammates had spent a lot of time working on this project in their spare time, but they had full-time jobs. What's more, it was likely they would be pulled away for a mission pretty soon. It was just the way things worked in the Navy.

Yeah, and you're leaving them in a lurch, aren't you?

Finn pushed the thought away. Right now with his fucked up headspace, he was more of a liability than anything else. He looked over at the passenger seat. He had his computer tablet with him. He wasn't anywhere close to the expert that Rylie, Clint or Lydia were on the computer, but he'd copied all of the information they'd had on the remaining unsolved missing baby cases.

If Declan's 'project' wasn't the missing babies, then he would show him the information he had, ask for some help, and be on his merry way.

———

FINN SPENT the night in Fredericksburg before heading into Austin. He'd gotten in some Physical Training, and was starving by the time he hit town. Craving Tex-Mex, he headed for Sixth Street when the phone rang.

"You in town?" Declan asked.

"Don't you have me tracked to within an inch of my life?"

"Maybe," Declan conceded. "I thought you'd like a semblance of privacy. So you're headed to Sixth Street. Want a beer?"

"Food, man. I'm hungry."

"I know just the place." Declan gave him directions. "There's even shaded parking for your baby."

"Is the beer Pacifico?"

"Nah, we'll be drinking Texas beer."

"Fuck, not Shiner Bock. That's all Jack ever talks about," Finn bitched, thinking about his teammate Jack Preston.

"Suck it up. I'll see you in twenty minutes." The phone went dead. Finn shook his head and continued toward the most popular street in Austin.

There was one shaded parking spot waiting for him when he pulled up to the cantina—amazing. Declan McAllister was one spooky dude. He locked his El Camino and admired the sky blue paint job. She was one of the few things that still gave him a certain amount of pleasure. It was sad when a car was the only thing that even came close to making him happy. Drake was right, he needed to pull his guilt-ridden head out of his ass, but he had no earthly idea how to do it.

He opened the door of the restaurant and was hit by a wave of air conditioning. After the humidity outside, he didn't care what he had to drink, the cool air made it worth it.

He spotted Declan at the far table with his back against the wall. He scowled, realizing he'd left him to sit with his own back toward the restaurant. He hated that position. Declan grinned knowing why Finn was irritated.

"Asshole," Finn said as he arrived and angled the table so they both could sit against the back corner of the restaurant walls.

"Paranoid much?" Declan asked.

A waitress came over and asked in English, what they would like to drink. When Finn asked for a Pacifico, he was offered a Shiner Bock instead. Declan flashed him a grin.

"That'll be fine," Finn said in Spanish.

"Make it two," Declan also said in Spanish.

She gave a wide smile and said she'd be right back with chips and beers. While they waited, Declan looked Finn over like he was a bug under a microscope.

"What? Are you considering dating me?"

"You look like shit."

"Thanks. You look tan. Actually, you look good." Finn was gratified to see that his friend looked so much better than the last time he had seen him. He winced as he remembered the hospital visit.

"Stop, I'm not there anymore."

"Quit reading my mind. My head, my space. Remember?" Finn said as he circled the top of his head with his finger. "Of course, it was an easy guess." It had been pretty harrowing when Declan had been in that hospital. The only positive was he had been so drugged up he probably didn't remember much.

"Quit with the morose thoughts, you're the problem child now."

"You still haven't told me why you're so tan. Where the hell have you been?" Finn asked.

"None of your business."

"Oh cut the crap. You're not in Army Intelligence anymore. Now you're running your own damn super-spy agency, and you know I don't have anyone to tell your secrets to, so spill it."

"Paraguay."

There was major flooding killing and displacing people down there, and he should have known the Shadow Alliance would be in the thick of things. But Declan?

"I thought you did intelligence gathering. I didn't know you were on the ground."

"I'm wherever they need me. It's a clusterfuck of epic proportions, so I've been there."

"If they needed you there, what are you doing here?"

"Because you look to be a clusterfuck of epic proportions."

"It's not that bad."

"When Finn Crandall decides to a request a discharge from his cherished team, it's bad."

"I'm on leave," Finn corrected.

"Only because Clint is good at forging your signature, don't try to bullshit me," Declan set down his beer with a thud. "I can't stay long."

"Good. I don't need a fucking babysitter."

"I did back then, so I'm returning the favor. Can you tell

me what happened? You know you need to get it off your chest."

Finn gave him a cold stare.

Finally, Declan settled back and crossed his arms.

"For fuck's sake, you already read every single document associated with the mission. Why are you asking me questions?" Finn exclaimed.

"Because I want to hear it from you. Because I'm serious. You need to talk about it."

"What? That's what they taught you? Did you have sex after your share circles?" Finn regretted the words as soon as they were out of his mouth.

"I'm sorry, Dec."

"Forget it."

"No seriously, I was out of line."

"You were, Crandall." He winced. Dec never called him by his last name.

"You have to forgive me. Nobody wanted you to get better more than I did. You needed those group sessions."

"I said leave it alone." Declan's eyes were emerald ice.

The waitress brought the beer, chips, and three different types of salsas. She also brought some homemade flour tortillas and butter. Each man placed their order, then waited until the waitress was out of ear shot before continuing their conversation.

"Dec?"

"Look, Finn, you're fucked in the head. Been there, have the T-Shirt. We're fine, until we aren't again, then we'll be fine again. But I will beat the shit out of you if you go too far."

Finn breathed a sigh of relief. "So why Austin?"

Declan set down his tortilla and snagged his beer. After

taking a sip, he took out his phone. He pulled up a file and showed it to Finn. "Look familiar?"

Finn grabbed the smartphone out of his friend's hands and went through all of the information. They were the records of the five births of the missing babies . They contained the names of the birth mothers, sex of the baby, APGAR score, weight, time, and date of birth. The only details on the people who bought the babies were the dates they picked up the kids, the amount they paid, and the city they had flown in from.

"I've read all of this before. What's your point?"

"One of your five mothers is here in Austin."

This was news to him. He had all of the records he had pulled from the team's computers. Even though he hadn't been to any of the brainstorming sessions in the last couple of weeks, they knew he was interested in the progress of reuniting the mothers and the babies.

"Are you sure of your information?"

Declan raised his eyebrow. Stupid question, of course, Declan was sure.

The waitress came to the table with their entrees.

"Which of the girls?" Finn asked before taking a bite.

"Dasha."

"I don't get it. Rylie and Lydia managed to reunite her with her great-uncle, and they were living in New York."

"Apparently, you're not the only one who wants to be off the grid. Sergei and Dasha are here in Austin. They're staying with an old friend of his named Lou Donatelli. He used to own a private detective agency here in Austin."

"But Dasha knows we're searching for her daughter."

Declan was eating and couldn't talk; he indicated Finn should try his food. He forked a bite of the *carne asada* and thought he might be having an orgasm. He had never tasted food this good. Talking would have to wait.

Finally, Declan began to talk again.

"We're looking into it, but it has to do with her past in the Ukraine."

"Well, no shit Sherlock. Glad to see the Shadow Alliance is living up to its hype."

"Fuck you," Declan said without heat. "We're still trying to get to the bottom of things. Anyway, Dasha took a powder a week ago, and your Scooby Squad hasn't noticed it yet."

Quicker than the eye could see, Finn's deadly K-Bar knife was resting on the table. "I like you and all, but if you refer to anybody on my team, or their wives in such an insulting way again, we might need to go outside and have a lesson in manners."

"Wound tight much?"

"Are. We. Clear?" Finn ground out the words.

Declan's emerald green eyes looked at him, not with fear, and not with hesitation. Instead, they were filled with compassion.

"We're clear, my friend." Finn blew out a long breath and put the knife away.

"But if you were thinking clearly, you would know how highly I regard you and each member of Midnight Delta. You know I intend to recruit each and every one of you. It's my hope the Navy will fuck things up, and you'll want to leave."

"Don't bet on it."

"If not your men, then Rylie and Lydia."

"Oh yeah, that'll happen." Finn could just see Clint and Darius taking out *their* knives. "So tell me about Lou Donatelli."

"Lou Donatelli is retired. His granddaughter is

investigating the case of Dasha's missing baby. She runs the PI firm now."

"Seems to me that if I go directly to Dasha, she'll just run again."

"That's my assessment," Declan agreed.

"So the detective agency and Dasha. What angle are you thinking?" Finn asked.

"I'd be pretty damn cautious. I think Angie Donatelli would welcome any and all help. From everything I've gathered , she's a straight shooter."

Finn pulled out his wallet.

"I've got this," Declan said as he took out his wallet. "I'm a civilian and making way more than you these days."

"Okay, you pay. I've still got to pay for a motel."

"I've got you one of the Alliance apartments. It sucks. But it'll do."

"What do you mean it sucks?"

"I mean it was furnished by one of those staging companies for when you're going to sell a house. Plenty of fake plants, fake fruit in bowls and little bathroom soaps in dishes."

Finn shuddered. "I'll grab a motel."

"You'll be here for a while, take the apartment. It has a junior Olympic swimming pool."

"Sold."

"Don't use the soaps." Finn shot his friend the finger. "Seriously, though, it's ready to move in, including food."

NOW THAT HE was past security, Finn jogged up the narrow staircase, eschewing the elevator that must have been installed in the thirties. He loved the old building. The wood and ornate plaster fixtures were amazing. He made his way down the hallway to the double doors marked Donatelli Agency and let himself in.

It was his lucky day, a woman in a red pencil skirt was on all fours obviously fighting with some wiring underneath the reception desk. Why she was working on it from the front, instead of behind the desk was beyond him, but he sure as hell wasn't going to bitch about it.

"Sarah, did you get Howard's toolbox?"

Her skirt wasn't too short, it covered everything it should, but it showcased everything else perfectly.

"Dammit, Sarah, I need some help down here. If you didn't get his toolbox, maybe some pliers?"

"I'm not Sarah."

Her head hit the bottom of the desk with a loud thunk.

"Ow!"

She started to crawl backward. Lord have mercy.

Finn was there in a shot and helped her to her feet.

She put her hands on his chest and pushed away, then scooped a mass of curls out of her face. She looked up at him. "Okay, that's more than a little embarrassing. Hi, I'm Angie Donatelli. Normally, I introduce myself to people face-to-face, not face to uhhhm." She waved behind herself, trying to interject a little humor into the situation. Finn raised an eyebrow.

"This would be the point you introduce yourself."

Shit. "Finn Crandall."

"Hello, Finn Crandall." She smiled, peeked around him and frowned. He turned and saw an empty doorway.

"What's wrong?"

She looked down, and he saw her look at his hand. "I know you're here for a reason, but I'm kind of in a bind. Can I ask for a favor?"

He stared at her.

"You're not much of a talker, are you? Look. I screwed things up under the desk. The landline isn't working as a result. There's this bolt that's too tight, and Sarah was supposed to be here with a toolbox and a pair of pliers fifteen minutes ago."

What the hell.

"Sure."

"I'll show you which one."

She knelt down gracefully and motioned him toward the desk. He stepped back in panic, waiting for the inevitable flashback to the farmhouse, but instead he was in the present, seeing lush dark auburn curls and a white blouse that exposed a lacy bra. There was no mistaking this woman in the red skirt for anything but a lush vision and the first thing to get his motor running in months.

"Finn?"

He knelt down.

It was a tight squeeze. She smelled good. Like strawberries. She pointed to the bolt, and he easily took it off.

"Anything else?"

"Nope." He watched as she expertly re-ran the landline wire where it needed to go.

Finn heard the door open and put his hand over Angie's head.

"I have the toolbox!"

Angie's head jerked up, but his hand was above her, and she hit it instead of the desk. She smiled her thanks.

They backed out from under the desk.

"I take it you didn't need the toolbox after all?" The middle-aged woman smiled at Finn.

"Nope, I managed to find a volunteer," Angie said, making Finn notice her Southern accent for the first time.

"Okay then. I'll be able to get ahold of CiCi. Are you a new client?" Sarah asked.

"I need to talk to Ms. Donatelli about a few things."

"Please, call me Angie."

"Finn, do you drink coffee?" Sarah asked.

"Yes, ma'am."

"I'll bring in two. Angie, I'll tell CiCi you'll get back to her a little bit later, does that sound good?"

"Thanks, Sarah."

"Don't mind her mess," Sarah said to Finn. "Our conference room is being painted, if it weren't for that, you would never see her office."

"Follow me," Angie said as she led him down a little hallway. It was no hardship following the sway of the red skirt. The smell of strawberries still lingered in the air.

He was overwhelmed when he reached her office and saw the disarray. Actually, the term disarray was mild. Chaos was better.

"I thought tornados only hit the panhandle."

"It's not that bad, is it? Sometimes we get tornados here in the hill country. But no, this is our attempt at getting organized. Just put them anywhere," she said indicating the stack of files on the chair.

"Aren't your files computerized?"

"These are Dad and Pops' old files. Sarah and I are in the process of getting them on the system. Dad's aren't too bad, but Pops' are illegible and read more like a Raymond Chandler detective novel than actual case notes."

Finn rubbed his chin.

"So why are you here?"

"I'm here about Dasha Koval."

"Dasha who?" Angie asked nonchalantly. Finn's eyes narrowed.

"What's up?" Sarah asked as she brought in two mugs of coffee.

"Nothing. Thanks for the coffee." Sarah took the hint, left the office and shut the door.

"If it makes you feel any better, I'm not here in any real official capacity. I take it she doesn't want the government to know she's here, right?" Finn used his most reassuring tone.

"Finn, I like you. You seem like a nice man. Why don't we have a nice cup of coffee, talk about the weather, and then you leave?"

"Look, I can help you find Dasha's baby," he said with a coaxing smile.

"Dasha who?" If Finn hadn't gotten the information from Declan he would have believed her, she was that believable.

"Dammit, this is serious." He barely kept himself from slamming his hand on her desk.

"I take client confidentiality seriously." Her brown eyes glittered.

"It seems to me you should take helping your clients just as seriously. I know she's working with you. I know your grandfather and Sergei Koval served together in Vietnam. I know Dasha is here and wants you to find her baby. I can help. I have information."

"Okay, so you don't get any coffee. Please leave." Her smile was all teeth, as she waved her hand in dismissal.

"And how to you plan to make me leave?" Finn folded his arms across his chest.

Angie continued sipping her coffee, opened her top drawer and carefully pulled out a Glock 9mm pistol and put it on her desk, never once taking her hand off of it. He approved.

He was getting closer and closer to smiling.

"All right," she instructed. "Tell me your story. Start with who you are. Please keep in mind, I've never liked fairy tales."

"I'm one of the Navy SEALs, who was on the mission that helped rescue Dasha and the other girls in British Columbia. How much did Dasha tell you about her rescue?"

"Up in Canada? She talked about a crazy man unlocking their cabins and trying to put them on boats."

"I don't understand, why was the man crazy?"

"Apparently, he was laughing, but he had tears on his face. Dasha and the other girls in her cabin knew one of her roommates was giving birth that night, and she insisted on seeing her. The crazy man finally took her to the clinic. There was another man there, holding the baby, and comforting Dasha's friend. Dasha said both men were warriors, but crazy. Dasha said the doctor was dead on the floor of the clinic."

"So she didn't just get on the boat like she was told, huh?" It did Finn's heart good to know the girls still had so much fight left in them after having been captives for so long.

"Not Dasha. So tell me more of your story."

"The crazy men were my teammates. Anyway, it was the end of a long operation that started in Mexico over a year ago."

"Doesn't seem like it's ended, if Dasha's baby is still missing."

"Point taken. There are actually five babies still missing."

"Five? Five girls like Dasha have had their children stolen from them?"

"A hell of a lot more than that. But five are still missing, the others have been reunited with their children." Finn watched Angie's look of anguish.

"I didn't realize. I thought everyone had been found." She bit her lip. For a moment he thought he saw tears forming, but then she blinked, and her hand gripped her gun tighter. "Those bastards. I've been working off the information Dasha and Sergei gave me, but it is pretty convoluted. They've been so adamant that I couldn't contact the government. I've been flying blind until my friend comes through."

"What do you mean, 'until your friend comes through?'"

She put her gun back in her desk drawer and leaned forward, resting her arms on her desktop. Suddenly, she looked more vulnerable than she had, and it wasn't because of the lack of a gun. She was truly upset by his information.

"I have a friend that I tapped to dig deeper into this Canadian take-down. I need to understand how the babies were sold."

"I've got all of the information my SEAL team has collected. How about we work together?"

"You still haven't told me your story. Why are you here? Why do you want to help me?"

"My team and I want to help all five of the girls find their babies. Right now, they're focused on the other four girls. I want to work with you on Dasha."

"Without involving the government? She is fanatical about that."

"Doesn't that raise some red flags to you?"

"She's a victim. I couldn't care less why she doesn't want to involve the American government. From what Sergei *did* manage to explain, they hadn't been helpful. He said since Dasha was Ukrainian and this happened in

Canada, the United States was washing their hands of the whole thing."

"That's not true," Finn said. "I do agree there was some bungling because of the jurisdictional issues, but they are definitely working the case."

"Then why are you involved?" Angie asked.

"Because we can't let a mission go uncompleted. There isn't a chance in hell we're going to stop looking for these babies."

"I would feel the same way," she said determinedly. "Are they all in the same place, or have they been adopted out to different people?"

"Different people."

"The United States?"

"That's what our records show."

"What records?"

"Lady, are we working together, or not?"

"We're working together. Let's get going, we might as well meet Dasha now. We need to get to the park."

"The park?" he asked as he followed her out of her office.

"Sarah, we'll be back in about two hours. We'll grab something at the sandwich shop, can we pick you up anything?"

"Pulled pork and some coleslaw."

"Corn on the cob?" Angie asked.

"You know it." Sarah reached for her purse, and Angie waved her hand as she headed out the door.

ANGIE WAS STILL TRYING to get a sense of Finn as they walked down the tree-lined street. She prayed he would be able to give Dasha some hope. In the last week, the girl had crawled into a place nobody could reach.

"You're going to have to treat her with kid gloves," Angie warned after they had gone a block in silence.

He stopped on the sidewalk, and she backed up a step to turn and look at him. "Lady, I haven't the slightest idea what you're talking about. I offered to show you records of our investigation, and you said we needed to go to the park. So far the only logical thing you've done is pull a gun on me."

"I'm sorry, you're right. I get this way sometimes. Can we keep walking? My grandfather and Sergei play chess in the park and have lunch. Dasha watches. It's a neutral setting, and I think it would be a good place for me to introduce you." Damn, she should have explained it sooner.

He nodded. "That makes sense."

"I think you're just the thing she needs. She has totally shut down. Having someone like you meet with her, could be just what the doctor ordered. She needs a hero."

She saw his expression shut down.

"Did I say something wrong," she asked as she gently clasped his wrist.

"Huh?"

"I got the feeling I upset you with what I said."

"You're imagining things. Do you have any advice on how I should approach her?" Angie hesitated. Something had bothered him. It couldn't have been that Dasha needed him, it was the reason he was here, so it had to be the hero comment. But why would that bother him?

"Angie," he prompted.

"Right now she's barely talking. The last two times she's seen me, she hasn't even asked about her baby. I think she's given up hope."

"I'm surprised she's at the park," Finn said.

"Sergei forces the issue. He's a good uncle."

"He's the only family she has, right?" Finn asked.

"Yes." Angie sighed. Another pedestrian walked by them. Angie spotted a bench near the park entrance. "Let's sit there and figure out our game plan before we see them."

"Is Sergei going to be okay with me showing up?" Finn asked as he put his hand on her back and led her to the bench. Angie noted how he brushed off the seat for her. It was a little thing, but it warmed her.

"Sergei is going to be fine with anything that helps his grand-niece get her baby back. I can tell he's feeling helpless."

"Do you know why she ran away? People were trying to help her find her baby. Not only her but the other four mothers. She knew this. Why would she leave New York and not tell anyone where she was going? It doesn't make any sense to me," Finn said.

"I don't know. I'm not sure Sergei even knows." Angie sighed.

"Okay." Finn's blue eyes stared intently at her. "Can you tell me how she and her uncle ended up here in Austin?"

"Sergei and my grandfather have known each other since they served together in Vietnam. They took a bus out here. They've been staying at Pops' ranch. Sergei promised Dasha that Pops would be able to help find her daughter, and that's when I was brought in."

Angie remembered meeting the distraught teenager who was by turns shy and frantic. If it weren't for Sergei as a stabilizing influence, Angie was sure the poor girl would have flown apart.

Her fist clenched as she remembered when she had first been introduced to Dasha. "Finn, she still hasn't recovered from giving birth. When I met her, she wasn't eating properly, and she wasn't getting the sleep she should."

Finn picked up her fist and gently pried it open. "You did something about that, didn't you?"

"I told her if she didn't take care of herself, she would end up going to the hospital. She didn't seem to care until her uncle said the government could find her that way. Then she went into a full-blown panic attack. He was relentless. But in the end, she agreed to start taking care of herself. That was when I realized she was afraid of the government finding her."

"What did you do?"

"I contacted a friend of mine to dig up everything he could find out about the operation to rescue Dasha. I figured anything I found out about the human trafficking ring or baby selling would help me assist her."

They sat there in silence watching the people walk by. "I still have trouble wrapping my head around all of this ugliness happening. I've read about it in the newspapers and watched documentaries, but to meet with a girl who's gone through it? It just blows me away."

Finn squeezed her hand in comfort. Angie looked down to where their hands were linked.

"Logically, I know that anybody who went to all the time and expense to buy a baby would have to be treating it well. It's the only thing about this that gives me comfort. I've actually cried about it." She pulled her hand away when she realized what she had admitted.

"Angie, there's no shame in that."

"Yes there is, I should be stronger," she said brusquely. She stood up. "Come on, let's go."

"Hold up." He reached for her hand and tugged her back down.

"What?" she demanded.

"Why do you think it's shameful you cried about Dasha's baby?"

"Because you just push past it, and get the job done." She gave him a hard stare and dared him to disagree.

"I've cried," he said softly.

"About this? I bet you haven't." His face flushed. "See, I knew it."

"No, not about this, but other missions. Other victims," his voice was a whisper. "It's okay to need a shoulder to cry on."

Was he for real? "We need to go talk to Dasha." This time, he didn't stop her when she got up from the bench.

They made it to the part of the park where the picnic tables were. Off in one corner, the two senior citizens were playing chess. Dammit, Dasha was just staring into space.

"Angela!" her grandfather called out. She gave him a wave. He and Sergei gave Finn the once over, but Dasha barely even took note of the stranger in her midst.

"This is Finn Crandall. He was one of the SEALs who helped rescue Dasha. He wants to help find her baby." Dasha's head jerked up.

"Government?" Dasha said the word like it was a curse.

"I'm here to help," Finn said solemnly.

"Angie, you made a promise." Dasha gave her an accusing stare. Angie took heart, it was the most emotion she had seen from the girl in the last week.

"He is a good man," Angie promised and hoped she was telling the truth.

"Uncle," she called out. "We leave."

Sergei looked down at the chess board, ignoring his niece.

"Uncle," Dasha said plaintively.

He still did not look up. The girl sat back down and looked at Angie. "How he help?"

"He has records about where the babies went," Angie began. Dasha stood up so fast, she got tangled up between the bench and the table. Finn was around to their side of the table in a heartbeat and helped the girl to stand outside the fixed bench of the picnic table.

"You know where my baby?" Dasha demanded, clutching his arm? "Where my girl? Tell me now!"

Finn looked helplessly at Angie.

Fuck!

"Dasha, that's not what I meant. He has *some* information, more than I had. He doesn't know where the babies are."

"Tell me where my Yulia," she said. It was the first time Angie had heard her call her daughter by a name. Dasha was clawing at Finn's chest. "Tell me!" she yelled.

Fuck! She'd screwed up.

Angie watched as Finn blanched. They were in the middle of August in Texas, and she saw the man shiver. His lips moved, but Angie couldn't hear what he was saying, and apparently neither could Dasha.

"What? What say you?" the girl demanded.

"I'm sorry. I'm sorry. I'm sorry." He muttered over and over again, as he trembled. It was a litany that made no sense, and it finally got through to the angry young girl. She backed up and looked at him.

"What wrong?"

"I'm sorry." Over and over again, he couldn't seem to stop saying the words. Dasha turned to Angie, all anger had fled, and she looked like what she was, a frightened young girl who was out of her element.

"Help him, Angie."

"Finn?" She moved forward and rested her hand on his chest, in the exact spot where Dasha had been clawing at his shirt. She could feel his heart beating like a freight train.

"Finn?" His eyes finally focused on her. He gripped her hand tightly in both of his.

"Angie?"

"I'm here, Finn."

His breath sawed in and out. "Well okay then." She rested her other hand on his shoulder and felt him begin to relax.

They stood like that for a long moment, and then he stepped back, and she was staring into blue eyes that looked like they had seen the depths of hell. He let out a long breath.

"Thank you." He glanced over her shoulder at Dasha and winced. "I see I'm making great first impressions."

"You didn't pull a gun on her, so you're doing fine," she whispered so only he could hear.

"Well, there is that," he admitted.

Angie turned in his arms so that they could be facing Dasha together. "Honey, can you come here and let us explain what Finn can do to help you?"

The girl tentatively came to stand in front of them.

"Dasha, you reminded me of some of the girls I helped rescue in Canada. Seeing you so scared and angry brought back bad memories for me. I'm sorry I lost control."

Angie watched as Dasha worked to comprehend what Finn was saying. "You are like men who help rescue me. Many feelings when they save baby. They try to be strong, but they feel way deeply when holding baby they save."

"Huh? Finn, what is she talking about?" Angie twisted to look up at him.

"Darius and Mason delivered a baby. On the island

where the girls were being held captive, there were two people in charge who were basically monsters. They were doing a C-Section without anesthesia and were planning on letting the mother die. They only cared about the baby. The baby was in distress, and Mason and Dare saved both mother and child. They then rescued Dasha and the other girls from their locked cabins. Mase and Dare were pretty emotional."

"You have strong emotions," Dasha noted.

"Maybe I do. But I want to talk about how I can help you."

"You like other men." Dasha was determined to say her piece.

"Yes, they are my teammates."

"You good men?" Dasha asked.

"I try to be," Finn replied. Dasha gave Angie a questioning look.

"Yes, he is a good man," Angie reassured Dasha, as she elbowed Finn in the stomach.

"How you help?"

"Can we sit down?" Angie peeked around Finn and saw her grandfather and Sergei pretending to play chess. It was obvious they were closely monitoring the conversation.

"Yes," Dasha agreed. She sat back down. Angie sat next to her, and Finn circled the picnic table to sit across from the two of them.

"Dasha, do you remember Rylie and Lydia? They were the women who helped to find your uncle."

She nodded and smiled broadly. "Da! I mean yes. They are with your friends?"

"Yes. My team. They discovered records that told us how much money was paid for each child."

"Bastards," Pops muttered. Angie looked at her

grandfather who had given up all pretense of playing chess. They moved closer to her and Finn.

"What else do you know?" Sergei asked.

"Not much. We know what city each couple flew in from. According to the records, each was listed as a couple."

"Hot damn!" her grandfather cried.

"Unfortunately, it hasn't been as easy as you might think. There were sixteen births in all. Based on DNA testing, we were able to reunite eleven of the girls with their babies, but now we are left with the five most elusive couples."

"What do you mean?" her grandfather demanded. "You said you knew which city they flew in from. Figure it out from the airline records of who flew in solo, and then flew back with a baby. Dammit man, how hard can that be?"

"Easy Pops," Angie soothed her grandfather. "I'm sure that's what they did on the first eleven. There must be some issues with these last five, or they would have already done that."

"They probably took alternate forms of transportation back. Cars, or ferries to the US. Or just stayed in Canada until things died down."

"But you know what city they came from," Sergei protested.

"That could have been a red herring," Angie said. Everybody fell silent, knowing it was the truth.

"Okay, you help. How soon you find Yulia? Angie tell me they will be good to her. But I love her more. She needs me." Angie gave the young girl a hug. Dasha was stiff in her arms, and she knew why. She was close to falling apart and didn't want risk breaking down.

"I need your help," Finn said to the girl.

"How?"

"I need you to tell me everything that happened when they took your baby."

"How that help?"

"Any little thing you might remember could be important. When did you have your baby? How long before you were rescued?"

Angie watched as Dasha considered Finn's question. A tear ran down her cheek. "Eighty-two days ago they take my Yulia. She was so good and quiet in my arms. I held her all night. I was so tired, but I no sleep because they will take her from me when I shut my eyes." Two more tears dripped down Dasha's face. "Yulia is good baby. She not cry once. She smile and look at me with her green eyes. She know and love her mama." Dasha started to say something in Ukrainian.

Sergei translated.

"A woman came into her room in the cabin and took Yulia. Dasha wanted to fight, but she knew her daughter would end up being hurt, and she was too weak from giving birth."

Sergei said something to Dasha, who shook her head and she started crying violently. He sat down beside her. They talked over one another in their native language. It was clear Dasha felt guilty, and Sergei told her that she didn't have a choice. But then Sergei got enraged and turned to all of them.

"The woman who took my grand-niece, that bitch, she told Dasha her daughter would be going to a grand house with servants. She said she would be better off than if she stayed with some no-name whore."

Before Angie could speak, Finn stepped in.

"Dasha, your child couldn't ask for a better mother than you. Until she is back with you, Yulia will never get more love than she did those first few hours in your arms. She knew you, and she felt your goodness and love. We will find her and put her back in your care. You have my promise."

Angie looked at this big man who projected such strength of will and hoped for both his and Dasha's sake he would be able to deliver on that promise.

3

——

ANY HINT OF VULNERABILITY HE SAW EARLIER WAS GONE. Angie had a no-nonsense attitude when they got back to her office. She immediately demanded all his information, not just on the sale of the babies, but also on the entire human trafficking operation.

"Why do you want that?" he asked as he sat across from her in her office.

"Just show me what you have," she said as she impatiently waved at the computer tablet he was holding.

"Lady, I'm not showing you a damn thing until you explain why you want it." He would have shown her anything, but he was actually finding it kind of fun to yank her chain. *What the hell?*

"Because I'm trying to better understand the type of scum we're up against," she said with frustration. "I want to understand how they think, how they operate, how they would have set things up."

"But they're dead." Finn thought back to Liu's blood splattering on him. "Trust me, they're no longer an issue. It's the people who bought the babies we have to concern ourselves with."

She tilted her head and gave him a quizzical look. "Do you really believe that? From what you told me, those people were still alive when Dasha's daughter was sold and taken. Hell, we don't even know if she was taken to the US or another country. Those traffickers, what were their names?"

"Liu. Albert and Jiang Liu."

"The Liu's. They would have been helping to coordinate the sale and the entrance and exit of the babies. I want to know everything about those men."

"Fuck. I should have thought about that. I'm sure Rylie, Clint, and Lydia have."

"How are they connected to you? Do you have female SEALs?"

"There are six SEALs who comprise the Midnight Delta team. Four of my teammates have women. They–"

"Women? Isn't that a bit of an archaic term?" What was it about the way she drawled the word archaic that got his motor running, Finn wondered?

"Sophia is the wife of my lieutenant. Beth, Lydia, and Rylie are engaged to be married to Jack, Clint, and Darius. Lydia is phenomenal with computers and so is Rylie. They have worked on this case to try and stop the human traffickers. We met Rylie when she was working undercover to stop this operation on her own."

"Wait, she wasn't always working with y'all?"

"No, it's a long story. Suffice it to say, she was embroiled in stopping the Lius when we met her. But I'm getting off track. It's Clint, Rylie, and Lydia who have been doing most of the legwork on reuniting the mothers and children. But the last time I talked to them, they thought Dasha was still in New York. Why is Dasha so fanatical about not having the government work with her? I thought she liked Rylie and Lydia."

"Finn, I think she does like Lydia and Rylie. They're the ones who reunited her with her uncle. She doesn't trust governments, and I get the feeling it has something to do with her past in the Ukraine. As soon as she could, she and Sergei left New York."

"I still don't get it. Wouldn't she want to stay and see if someone could find out information about Yulia?"

"According to Sergei, some agents came and questioned her at his apartment. They came while he was gone. How she described them, they sounded like CIA or FBI. They scared the hell out of her. Dasha and Sergei left town the next day."

"This shit just keeps getting weirder. But I understand why you want the info on the Liu's. You're right, they would have been involved in getting Yulia smuggled out of Canada." Finn looked at Angie. She looked a little mussed up from their walk in the park, her curls were wild, and white blouse was molded to her body. She looked too innocent to hear all of the horrors of the trafficking.

"Why are you hesitating?"

"It's pretty ugly."

"I've worked on ugly cases in the past," she said calmly. "Unfortunately, this profession has allowed me to see the monsters in the closet."

"What's your e-mail?" She gave it to him. He pulled up the relevant files and e-mailed them to her. "This is enough to get you started. In the meantime, I'm going to go back to my apartment and start looking at this from the angle you just provided," he said as he stood up.

"Can I ask you something?"

He paused on his way to the door of her office. "Sure."

"Why are you here and not with your friends?"

"I needed some space," he clipped out the words. She got the message.

"Okay. When will I see you again?"

"Why don't you call me after you've had a chance to go over all of the information in the files. I figure you'll have questions, and we can discuss them."

He had one foot out the door when she said his name again. His shoulders slumped, and he turned around. "Yes?"

"This is a lot of information; it'll take me a while. I would like to talk to you before I'm done with it. Can we meet for dinner tomorrow?" She smiled at him calmly. She knew what she was doing. He'd made it clear that he needed space, but she was pushing to see him tomorrow night anyway. He sighed.

"All right."

"I need a way to reach you."

"You have my e-mail."

"What happens if something with Dasha comes up and I need to reach you immediately?" she asked sweetly.

He came back to her desk and grabbed a post-it and pen, and quickly scribbled on it. Then he pasted it on her computer screen. "Here's my IM and my phone number."

He walked out before she could stop him again. *Pushy woman.*

THERE WASN'T enough ice cream in the world to handle this. Angie sat on her loveseat with all of the lights on in her house. She had foregone the bowl and poured the chocolate syrup directly into the carton of vanilla ice cream. The faint taste of salt in the mixture, made her realize she was crying again. She set it aside.

"Sink, Angela," she admonished herself, as she saw the carton drip on her coffee table. She didn't give a shit, let it stain the wood. She wiped her eyes with the sleeve of her Texas Longhorn sweatshirt.

The notes had been put together by Lydia, Rylie, and Clint, and were for the Midnight Delta team members. However, they also included some of the official reports provided to Navy Command. It had gone back as far as when they first tracked the slavers in Mexico over a year ago.

There were no personal notes when it came to Lydia and Beth Hidalgo's involvement with the sex traffickers, but the official records explained how their original kidnapping in the Mexican jungle precipitated the case in British Columbia.

Later, there were comprehensive notes by Clint, Rylie, and Lydia detailing the operation in British Columbia. From Clint's perspective, it was so he could make a report to his commander. For the women, it was so they could best figure out how to help the girls assimilate after they were rescued.

Step by step, they outlined the horror of the human trafficking of women from all over the world. The operation in British Columbia might have been centered around Eastern European women, but what Angie read showed how South, Central, and North American women had been targeted as well. Also, there were Asian women who had been brought over in shipping containers. When Angie read the part where Jiang Liu had ordered one of shipping containers of women be shoved over the side of a cargo ship, she literally rushed to the bathroom to throw up. That had been this morning.

What had her crying tonight was when she realized the

Liu's had been at this for countless years. How many thousands of women had been bought, sold, and killed? How many babies had been ripped out of their mother's arms?

"Okay, Angela, you need to get it together." She threw the carton of ice cream in the sink. She looked at the clock over the stove. Just after midnight.

She thought long and hard. She really shouldn't need anyone to talk to. What was the family motto? Or at least the motto for little Angela? Suck it up, buttercup. You hold yourself up by your bootstraps. But maybe if she called to talk about the case he wouldn't realize that she was looking for comfort as well.

She'd take a chance. Worse thing that happened is he didn't answer. *Finn?* She typed into her instant message.

You okay, Angie? Came the immediate response. She sat there stunned. She read the words three times. Never in her life had someone, not even family, shown such immediate and unconditional concern. Then she shrugged it off. It was just because Finn was one of life's born protectors. It wasn't anything personal.

Fine. She paused. *Having some ice cream. Reading notes.*

Strawberry?

No. Vanilla with chocolate sauce. Why did you think strawberry?

Never mind. Why are you eating ice cream in the middle of the night? It's the reports, isn't it?

Yes.

She stared at the blank screen, wondering why it was taking him so long to respond.

Are you done reading everything?

Almost. I read Mason's report where you killed Albert, and Darius killed Jiang.

That made you need to eat ice cream?

God no. That was the first thing that made me smile. I'm the one that pulled a gun on you, remember? I'm a Texan. Of course, that made me smile.

Why are you eating ice cream in the middle of the night? Because I have a mother and a sister. I know this means you're upset.

She wasn't touching that question with a ten-foot pole.

Where would you like to go for dinner tomorrow? What do you like to eat? Angie asked, changing the subject.

Her phone rang.

She blew her nose before she answered it.

"Hello, Finn."

"We can eat fried mustard for all I care. Are you crying?" he demanded. His voice was deep and masculine, it had a hint of gravel in it. Given the right circumstances, his voice would make her shiver. Tonight she would take comfort from it.

"Answer me, Angie, are you crying?"

"Maybe," her voice wobbled.

"Tell me why."

"I started to calculate how long they had been in business..." her voice trailed off.

"I've tried not to think about it. I know Rylie looked for records, but she couldn't find any." She heard the pain in his voice.

"I like her. I like everybody I read about." She sniffed. "It's not like I haven't been in the middle of bad shit before. But there was always a beginning, middle and end. Even though sometimes those ends were horrific." Her voice broke on that last word.

"Angie? Are you okay?"

"I'm fine. Just another bad thing to think about. I guess

I'll be sleeping with all the lights on and the gun under my pillow. Not the first time. Look, I need to go."

"Don't hang up." She hesitated her finger over the 'end' button.

"I need to sleep, Finn. There's no reason for you to be up trying to console me. I'm fine really. Nothing that a good night's sleep won't fix." There, her voice had sounded almost perky.

"I hadn't really considered it, but you must sometimes see some bad shit as a P.I.," he said softly as if he had just considered it.

"Not on this scale." She had trouble keeping her voice from breaking.

"We got the bad guys. Take solace from that."

"I'm trying to." She twisted the sleeve of her sweatshirt.

"Did you find any new angles?" he finally asked.

"Not yet. I think I need a day or two to distance myself."
It was time to shut this shit down.

"What time should I pick you up for dinner?" Finn asked.

"Let's just skip it," she wouldn't be able to put on a happy face, and she hated the idea of him seeing her vulnerable.

"No way. I'll just hunt you down, now what time?"

Angie looked at her phone. She kept forgetting she was dealing with an alpha male. "I guess seven. Finn, can I ask you a question?"

"Sure."

"You don't smile. Is it because of all of this?" There was dead silence on the phone. After almost a minute, she finally spoke again. "So no comment on the smile question."

"I thought that was obvious," he said heavily.

"Thanks for the call, I'll e-mail you my address. Hopefully, we'll be able to smile at dinner."

IT WAS the first time in weeks that Finn was able to sleep. Maybe because he had something to actually look forward to. He got up the next morning, worked out, and then went for a fifteen-mile run. It felt like he was running through the jungle with the humidity. It was good for him, he thought as he gritted his teeth the last mile.

The team had been on six missions in the jungle since the harrowing one where they marched for five days carrying the Hidalgo's through Mexico. But every time Finn even thought the word jungle all he could think about was Beth and Lydia being brutalized by the men of the cartel. When he got to the apartment, he stripped off his sweat-drenched clothes and let the shower pound down on him, trying to remind himself that the two women were safe, protected, healed and loved.

After the shower, he had gotten himself together and grabbed a protein shake. He checked his e-mail to see if Declan had sent him any information regarding Dasha's case. He knew his friend, it wouldn't matter that he was in Paraguay, now that his curiosity was piqued he'd have his minions looking into Dasha's case. There wasn't anything this morning, but Finn knew eventually there would be something.

He sat down and continued to read through the files with a new perspective. Angie really was a genius. Not only would Liu have been involved in the selling of Dasha's child, but he would also have set up the network of selling the infants. Therefore, figuring out how he thought and operated would be integral in finding the five remaining buyers.

"I bet you're a good P.I.," Finn mumbled aloud.

He was taking notes, and not paying attention to anything besides his scribbling and the computer when his alarm rang.

"Fuck." How had it already come to be almost six p.m.?

He needed another shower, and his clothes needed to be ironed, but he hadn't found one in the apartment. He dragged his slacks and dress shirt into the bathroom with him and hoped that the steam would get some of the wrinkles out. He'd have to make a Target run at some point in the near future.

When he got dressed, he looked in the mirror and was satisfied with how he looked.

What the hell? This is a business dinner, Crandall, who cares how you look?

He grabbed his keys and headed for Angie's house. She lived in an older part of town that had been through a restoration. Her house was far back from the street and looked like it had been built in the thirties. As he walked up the steps, Finn could see that there were motion detectors on the property, of which he approved. Angie took her security seriously.

He knocked on the door, and she opened it. He was glad that he had chosen to dress up. She was wearing strappy heels and a fashionable sundress. She was a knockout.

"Would you like to come in?"

"Do you still have to get ready?" he asked.

"No. I like to be on time. But I figured you might like to take a load off, have a beer or something before we take off."

"Depends on what you have."

"I have friends from California. I have Shiner Bock, of course. I have Blue Moon, and I picked up some Pacifico today." He nodded in appreciation.

"I would love to come in and take a load off."

She grinned and ushered him in. He looked around and was surprised.

"It's neat."

"I really am kind of a neat freak. The office was an anomaly. Automating those files has been a bitch."

Finn liked the idea that she was organized. It made sitting down in her home more relaxing. She must have known because she grinned.

"Oh God, you're OCD too, aren't you?"

"I don't know what you're talking about." He watched as she headed over to the kitchen. He liked the open floor plan of the house, it allowed him to study Angie as she moved around. She was beautiful to watch.

She came back holding two beers.

"I didn't tell you which one I wanted," he said as she handed him the Pacifico.

"I'm an investigator. It's my job to know these things." She sat down beside him and started drinking her Shiner Bock, he liked that she drank from the bottle, it was sexy.

"Tell me about yourself, Finn."

"I'm from Minnesota originally."

"Do you like winters? Did you play ice hockey?"

"To a point, and yes."

"What do you mean to a point?" She set down her beer on a coaster and pushed one over for him as well.

"When winter would last for five months, it was no longer enjoyable." He took another sip of beer and watched her digest that information.

"Sounds like a Texas summer. After a month of living in air conditioning, it's no fun."

"Have you always lived in Texas?"

"I lived in Paris for a year. And no, not Paris, Texas, I

mean Paris, France." It was easy to imagine her drinking a glass of wine in a Parisian café with some man.

"What took you over there?"

Angie picked her beer back up and settled back against the couch. "A professor arranged for me to get a job over there. I worked as an assistant to a Texas lawyer. I was pre-law at U.T., and I had taken a couple of years of French as well."

"You were pretty young. Didn't you miss your family?"

"Pops came and visited me, but it was the same time as the Monte Carlos Grand Prix so I think that might have had something to do with it." He could hear the wistful tone in her voice. He put his hand on hers on the back of the couch. She looked up at him, startled.

"What about your parents?"

"They were busy." She hid it well, but he heard the sadness in her voice. "It was a great adventure." She took another sip of her beer and gave him a perky smile. It was fake, but he knew better than to call her on it, time to change the subject.

"When did you get into the family business?"

"When I came back from Paris." She smiled.

"You didn't go to law school?"

"Nah. After working for Barney, I realized I didn't want to be a lawyer. Too much structure. I'd been hearing stories from Pops for years about his cases. Dad was a lot more closemouthed. But Pops always talked. He didn't make it sound glamorous or anything, but he made it sound like you had to use common sense, and every day was a different challenge. I liked that."

"What did your dad say when you said you wanted to join the firm?"

"He said I needed to gain experience, and not with him. I went to work for Pinkerton."

"Isn't that the agency that was started in the eighteen hundreds?"

"Yep. They're international. I learned a lot. They sent me back to France on a couple of assignments. I stayed with them for five years. I was really looking forward to working with Dad, but in the end, he just retired and handed the reins to me. We never did end up working together," she said wistfully.

"He didn't train you personally?"

"Oh I'm sorry, I didn't mean it that way. He stayed with me for five weeks before retiring. He's now playing golf almost full-time. He said he wanted to do this while he still had a scratch handicap. Mom loves it, he plays all over the United States, and she calls herself his camp follower." Finn couldn't believe it. The man didn't give his daughter any more time than that? What the hell?

"Isn't he awfully young to have retired?"

"He's sixty-six. Finn, I'm thirty-four. I'm a lot older than you are."

"Not that much older. I'm twenty-nine," he protested.

She lifted her eyebrow. "Finn, think of all that I've done. I've lived in another country for a year. I'm five years older than you are. I own a company."

"Good point. After all, I've lived this sheltered life." He watched as Angie blushed.

"I don't know why I'm even saying any of this, we're here tonight to talk about Dasha and the case." Yeah, and he dressed up for no reason whatsoever. At least, he consoled himself with the fact that she had dressed up and had researched what beer to buy for him. He wasn't in this by himself.

"You're right, Dasha and the case. Where are we going to go for dinner?" he asked.

"You never did tell me what you liked to eat, so since I was hungry for steak, that's what we're having."

"I have never gone on a date where the woman wanted a steak."

"Well, here's the thing. We're not on a date. And you're in Texas. So you need to adjust your expectations."

"I guess I do." She held out her hand for his empty beer bottle. He handed it to her. She got up and put it in the kitchen along with her own. He stood up and waited for her by the door.

They stepped out onto the porch, and she reached into her purse and took out her keys. He held out his hand.

"What?"

"I'll do that."

"You'll do what?" she asked, clearly confused.

"Lock your door."

She laughed. "It's okay, I can do it."

"Humor me." She rolled her eyes and handed him her keys. He easily found her key to the door and locked it. Then he pocketed them.

"Aren't you going to give them back to me?"

"I will at the end of the evening. I'm going to unlock your door, and see you safely inside."

"Are you sure you're not from the south?"

"The boys down here have been doing this for you?"

"Hell no, they've tried, but I kind of scare them."

"I'm not surprised." He put his hand on her lower back and ushered her down the walk to his car. "I'm impressed with your security."

"Wait a minute," she stiffened under his hand. "You saw

that? Goddamit. You weren't supposed to be able to see that."

"Lady, it's my business to be able to see it. I would be dead a hundred times over if I couldn't spot different security measures."

Finn felt her relax. "I guess that makes sense." He unlocked his car door, and opened it for her, and handed her into the passenger seat. She let out a small laugh.

"What?"

"It's been about a hundred years since I've been out with a man and I haven't had to climb into a truck."

"I can imagine."

"I like this car. Let me guess, you did all the restoration yourself."

"Why do you say that?"

"It goes with the OCD. You would want all the control of having taken care of every aspect of the restoration."

"Hold that thought." He closed her door, and went to his side and slipped into the car. "You have a good understanding of the human psyche, don't you?"

"I damn well better. Otherwise, I would be in deep trouble." She pointed down the street. "Take a left at the stop sign. Then we're heading north on the highway. Take the first exit. I'll tell you where to go after that." Finn nodded.

Angie pointed out different spots along the way, explaining some of the tourist attractions as well as the local landmarks.

"That's the neighborhood where my grandmother's parents lived when I was growing up," she said pointing to an affluent neighborhood.

"So your mother's side was Texan, and your father's side was from New York?"

"Yep, New York Italian. Both Pops and Sergei actually enlisted in the marines in the early sixties. Later, after they got out, they were friends in New York. Later my Pops moved to Texas."

"That seems like quite a jump for a New York Italian marine to move to Texas."

Angie laughed. "It was. But my grandmother had spent the summer in New York with a friend of hers. He met her and fell in love. It was one sided. But that didn't stop him. He followed her to Austin. He joined the Austin Police Department. He courted her, and she fell in love with him. Her family disapproved until they had my dad. Once there was a grandchild, all bets were off."

"That's a great story."

"What about your family?"

"They're great," Finn said as he pulled into the parking lot of the steakhouse.

GOD, the man looked good in slacks, Angie thought as she stood back just a little to watch him give his name to the hostess. Don't ogle, she admonished herself. But seriously, who could blame her? Dammit! Had the hostess just caught her?

"Right this way," the hostess said, as she carried menus and ushered them toward their table. When Finn wasn't looking, she winked at Angie. Yep, she'd been caught.

Finn held out her chair, and Angie sat down.

The waitress came and took their orders.

"I'm sorry if coming to dinner was a bad idea, Finn. I know I said that I was going to take a couple of days to mull over everything I read, and tonight might be a bit premature. The first thing I want to do is apologize for coming off so needy on the phone last night."

"You didn't come off needy," he said gently.

"For God's sake, I cried."

"So?"

"I don't do tears."

"Angie, look at me."

She looked down at the roll on her plate and took a long time buttering the bread.

"Angie?"

It obviously needed more butter.

"Angie?"

More butter.

"Angie." She looked up. She didn't know that he had been in command. She thought he had been one of the guys who *took* orders. "That's better."

"What did you want?"

"I wanted you to look at me. I wanted you to believe me when I said you didn't come off across as needy. But you know something, if you had, I would have liked it. You needing me is appealing."

She looked at him like he had just grown a second head. "What did you say?"

"It's okay if you want to lean on me. For God's sake Lady, after everything you read, I would think that there was something wrong with you if you didn't need some comfort."

Hug. Last night. She'd needed a hug.

His blue eyes captured hers, and she felt herself falling into a lake of blue. A plate blocked her view as her food was placed on the table in front of her. She looked up at the waitress and gave a wan smile.

Finn reached over and put his hand over hers, and she found herself breathing easier.

"Let me know if I can get you anything else," the waitress said.

"Everything looks great," Finn said, but he wasn't looking at his plate, he was looking at her. Angie felt her cheeks heating. She could get used to his attention.

He let go of her hand, and they started to eat.

"I've done most of the talking so far, tell me about yourself. What made you join the Navy?"

"I always knew I wanted to be a SEAL. There was only one fly in the ointment. My best friend wanted to be an Army Ranger. We fought all through school. To this day he swears that Army Rangers are far superior to Navy SEALs."

"That's too bad that you couldn't serve together."

"At least I got to be stationed in San Diego. That is a huge plus," Finn said as he continued to plow into his steak. Angie had obviously chosen a good place for dinner.

"So how does he like being a Ranger?"

"That's the funny thing, he ended up being in Military Intelligence, which wasn't that big of a surprise. He's no longer in the Army."

"What happened?"

"Medical discharge," was Finn's clipped response. Angie took the hint and didn't question further.

"How about you, do you intend to retire from the Navy? Don't you just have to put in twenty years? How old were you when you enlisted?"

"Yes. Yes. Eighteen."

"Did you ever think of getting a degree?"

"Thanks to Uncle Sam, I've got one."

"Really? In what?"

"Supply chain management and logistics."

"That seems kind of odd."

His left lip quirked upwards. "Not really. Coordinating projects and missions is critical."

"So what is your rank?"

"Chief Petty Officer."

"Do you lead a team?" He finished off the final bit of steak and chewed. It was obvious he was thinking how to answer her question.

"Right now I'm in a perfect spot, with the best team imaginable. My lieutenant is the best one I could ask for. I wouldn't change a thing."

"Then why are you here now, instead of in San Diego?"

He took a sip of water. "You sure do ask a lot of questions."

"It's part of being an investigator. Do you want me to stop?"

"I guess I do."

"All right. How about some dessert?"

"Now that's a question I can answer."

ANGIE WAS IMPRESSED how Finn didn't make her feel uncomfortable. For the rest of the evening, they were able to find plenty of other topics of conversation. They both had a lot of interest in the foster care system. He explained about Rebecca, the girl his mother had taken in as a foster daughter last year.

"She's remarkable. I can't believe how resilient she is, and it pisses me off how easily she fell through the cracks."

"Unfortunately, I've seen some of my client's children end up in the foster care system when the spouses are slinging mud against one another."

"What do you mean?" Finn asked.

"Last year both spouses were saying that the other spouse was sexually abusing the two children. There weren't any other relatives for the kids to go to, so for six months they had to go into foster care while the courts figured out what the hell was going on."

"You have got to be shitting me?"

"I'm not. It was pathetic. I was finally able to assist the father in proving the mother's boyfriend had a history of pedophilia. The dad got custody back. Unfortunately, the kids ended up separated, and the little boy was put into three different homes in the six months he was in the system. It was because he was acting out so badly. Normally that wouldn't happen, it was just a bad set of circumstances all the way around. The boy is still in therapy."

"Rebecca's story definitely had a happy ending." He smiled. "What kind of cases do you normally have?"

"Because we have been in business almost fifty years here in Austin, we have an established clientele. I'm on retainer with three different corporations, and that makes up seventy percent of my business. So it's really boring."

"Really? You have a gun in your desk."

"I'm a Texas girl. Do you know how many of us have carry and conceal?"

"A lot?"

"You could say that," she grinned. "Anyway. The cases that aren't boring are really not boring."

"Dangerous?" he asked as he took a sip of his dessert coffee.

"There have been a couple that have been dicey over the years."

"How much training have you had?"

"I'm an expert marksman. I've had extensive martial arts

training. I take this seriously Finn." She watched him give her an assessing glance, especially looking over her arms. She held up her right arm and flexed.

"Satisfied?"

"Not really. But it's not bad."

She rolled her eyes and picked up her purse to pay.

"I'm paying." He already had his card on the table.

"This is business. I can write this off."

"I checked out your cleavage. Therefore, I'm paying." She looked up at him from under her lashes. She hadn't been sure if the chemistry had all been one sided or not. Apparently not. *Good.*

FINN WAS of two minds as he led Angie up the walkway to her door. He was still mentally kicking himself and reminding himself that he did not mean for this to be a date.

And if this was a date...really? I checked out your cleavage? What, was he? In fucking junior high school?

Then there was the other part of him that wanted to take her in his arms after hearing all the things that she had told him. Like when he had heard the story of her parents not visiting her in Paris, and her Dad basically deserting her to run the business alone, he'd begun to see a pattern. As tough and capable as she was, there was a part of Angie that had been abandoned. No wonder she always felt she needed to be strong and tough.

He unlocked the door for her, and she checked her alarm system which was secure.

"Would you like to come in?" she asked shyly.

"I better not."

"Okay," she bit her lip and gave a bright smile. "So,

maybe the day after tomorrow will be a better time to discuss the reports?" He watched her hands twist her little red purse.

Dammit, he'd just rejected her. What was he thinking?

He reached out and dug his hand into the curls like he had wanted to three days ago. God, her hair was as soft as he had imagined. As he bent close, he smelled strawberries. Was it her shampoo? Her lip gloss? Damn, when she had reapplied the gloss in his car, he had almost drooled.

He touched his lips against hers. So soft. She flowered open and sighed. Her hands stopped twisting her bag, and instead crept up and circled around his neck. He tasted the sweetness that was Angie, loving the way that melted against him. He felt a little sting at his neck, and realized her nails were biting into his nape, he reciprocated, by tugging at her hair. She groaned and pressed closer.

There was something so fresh and freeing about Angie. She brought a little bit of light to some of the dark places in his soul. He pulled back so he could look into her brown eyes, needing to see her desire.

"Finn," she whispered.

He dipped back down and trailed kisses from her jaw to her neck.

"So good," her voice was just a puff of air.

He had to look at her again. It was a deep seated need for him to make sure she was with him every step of the way.

"What?" she asked.

"Do you want this? Really want this?" He watched as she bit her lip.

"Tell me, Angie. Tell me true." A phrase from his childhood.

"Yes." She paused. "No." Another pause. She looked up into his eyes. "I don't know. I'm so sorry."

"Shhh. Lady, it's fine." He bent his head, touching his forehead to hers. "Nothing is more important to me than honesty. I wasn't planning on this either. I don't think I'm ready, and now that I know you're not one hundred percent with me, I *know* I'm not ready."

He saw her relieved look. He brushed back the hair from her face, luxuriating in the softness of her curls.

"I love your hair."

"That's because you don't have to tame it every morning."

His eyes glinted. "I notice you haven't cut it, Ms. Donatelli." He smirked.

"God save me from perceptive men."

"Okay, get inside. I'll wait out here until you've locked your door and set your alarm."

She shook her head. "Paranoid much?" An echo of Declan's words. Interesting.

"I prefer to think of it as cautious."

He watched as she closed the door, and he listened for the lock and the arming of the alarm. He took a deep breath before walking down the walkway to his car. For a moment a smile hovered. He had forgotten what is was like to be so hot and bothered by a woman. Then pictures and events slammed through his mind, and all the good feelings that Angie had evoked, fled.

His hand fisted on the top of his car. Dammit, what was he thinking? He shouldn't be touching someone as good and kind and wonderful as Angie Donatelli. He slammed his fist down on the steel. The pain felt good. He deserved pain. He got in the car and drove into the night.

4

Angie waited until Thursday to have time to process the reports. Then she called Finn. When she got voicemail, she left a breezy little message about the files and asked him to call her. By the next day, she couldn't decide if she was pissed or hurt he hadn't called back. But because she believed in honesty, she had to admit she was eighty-three percent hurt.

"Who peed in your Special-K?" Sarah asked as she handed Angie another set of completed notes that she'd entered into the database.

"Sarah, the term is 'pissed in your Wheaties.'"

"You say it your way, I'll say it mine. I'm betting it was Finn. I'll be right back." Angie watched as Sarah left the office, knowing what was coming. Seconds later, in came the Tupperware.

"You didn't," Angie said as she reached for the container. Sarah handed her a spoon.

"Honey, you *so* need sugar. Especially with your mom in Ireland, you haven't had anyone to cook for you." They looked at one another and laughed. The idea of Emily Donatelli cooking was pretty damn funny.

"Well, they seem to be enjoying their time, even though dad isn't placing well in the tournament."

"Bet your mom is still managing to find things to buy."

"Undoubtedly," Angie agreed.

"So tell me what's going on between you and Finn."

"Nothing," Angie said quickly.

"We can do this the easy way, or we can do this the hard way."

"What's the hard way?" Angie asked curiously.

"The next time Brad calls, I'll tell him you secretly want to get back together with him, and you're just playing hard to get."

"Sarah!"

Sarah gave her an evil smile.

"You wouldn't actually do that, would you?" Now Angie was curious.

"No, I wouldn't. The man is dumb as rocks and needs to go back to his wife and daughter. The two of you were over years ago. He's just run into a hiccup in his marriage and thinks that he can call you up. He's a dumbass."

"I don't get it. He wasn't always. He was so sweet when we were engaged."

"You didn't dump him for being stupid?"

"God no." Angie bit the end of her pen. "Well, maybe a little. I don't know. There just wasn't that spark. Pops loved him. When Pops went to buy a new computer, Brad helped him install all the software that he wanted."

"I remember. Your grandfather would snap his fingers, and he'd come running," Sarah said as she snapped her fingers.

"It wasn't that bad."

"Yes, it was. He did it on purpose, he wanted you to realize that he wasn't the guy for you. He had jellyfish tendencies."

"What?"

"He was spineless."

"Stop. I was engaged to the man for two years. He was funny, nice, and way back when he was loyal to a fault. Yes, he was and always has been, a follower. That doesn't mean he's spineless."

"Bullshit, one of the reasons you fit so well together was that he was looking for someone to make his decisions for him."

Angie dropped the food container on her desk, the spoon clattered.

"Well, I hated it! It wouldn't have been so bad if he had just once in a while asked about my day and been there for me when I needed him. Instead, it was always about his needs."

"How'd you end up breaking up with him?"

"I told him we weren't ready for the same things. Apparently, I left a window open."

"A window he keeps trying to crawl through."

"He's married for God's sake!" Angie cried.

"His wife kicked him out of her window."

Angie looked at the dessert. The peach cobbler had lost its appeal. "I can't eat anymore. Thanks for bringing it in, though."

"Angie, I'm sorry. I didn't mean to bring you down. I was just teasing about Brad."

"I know, but I screwed up with Finn too. Do you realize it's been almost a year since I've been on a date, and I can't even get the man to call me back? And, and, and..."

"And what?"

"And, I sound like a junior high school girl. For God's sake, we agreed to talk in two days. It's been three. Here I am stressed about it. I'm a dumb shit." Angie sighed. "Okay. That's what was really bothering me. Not so much that Finn didn't call, but that I was bothered by it."

"So you like him. There's no harm in that. Like you said, you haven't gone on a date in over a year. I've watched you, Angie Donatelli, since Brad, you've been really picky."

"I'm not picky. Nobody has been interested."

Sarah snorted. "Seriously? You're seriously going to say that to the woman who has to field your phone calls?"

"Okay, nobody suitable has asked me out."

"So we're back to picky."

"Anyway," Angie interrupted and tried to change the direction of the conversation. "I'm just saying, I'm an idiot for getting so twisted up about not getting a call."

"I don't blame you for you feeling a little rejected that he hasn't called. But your instincts are right, it's no big deal."

"Okay. Thanks, I still feel dumb for needing reassurance."

"I'm just excited you like him. So tell me about the date."

"Well first we kind of agreed it wasn't a date, but then he kissed me."

"If there was a kiss, then it was a date. Tell me more." Sarah pushed some of the papers out of her way and propped her elbows on the desk.

"We went to Ray's Steakhouse. When I tried to pay for the meal, he said he'd pay because he'd checked out my cleavage."

Sarah laughed. "So our boy Finn has class." Angie rolled her eyes.

"Anyway, he told me later that checking out cleavage constitutes a date, so he kissed me."

"You already told me that, and we'll circle back to it. I want to hear more about what went on during dinner."

"We talked about the case."

"Not that kind of stuff. Tell me about the date part."

"He's young." Angie looked down to where she was biting the tip of her thumb again. She shoved her hand under her desk.

"He looked over the age of consent to me."

"That's not funny." And it wasn't. Five years was a big deal. Not if the guy was older than the girl, but it sure as hell was a big deal if the girl was older than the guy.

"I'm sorry, honey. Okay, how much older are you?"

"He's twenty-nine."

"You have to know that's really not a big deal. You mentioned he was a Navy SEAL. That's not some small time career. That is someone who has been through the fire. It ages you. I'm not sure you can really just say he's twenty-nine. Because, honey, you're not just thirty-four either. He needs a grown-up, and you need a grown-up."

She looked at her friend and saw the sincerity on Sarah's face. It settled her down. The woman had a point.

"What else?"

"I invited him inside."

"Going right for it, were you?" There was no judgement, just a friendly smile. God she loved Sarah.

"But he asked if I was really ready, and I told him I probably wasn't. He said we should wait until I was." Sarah cupped her chin and sighed.

"I think I'm in love for you."

"I know, right?" Angie's eyes glowed. "But now the jerk hasn't returned my phone call. He said we would talk yesterday, so I called yesterday. I still haven't heard from him."

"Now I understand who pissed in your Wheaties."

"Exactly."

———

FINN'S first instinct that morning had been to work out to the point of exhaustion as he had for the last three days. But instead, when he woke up he heard the birds, and rather than grating on his nerves like a jackhammer, it sounded kind of pleasant. He got up and found he didn't have to choke down breakfast. He actually enjoyed the toast—especially the strawberry jam.

He closed his eyes and gave thanks. He hated it when he had these dark episodes. It had been the Angie kiss. But now he remembered it with something that felt like pleasure. As soon as he thought about it, he decided he needed a shower and a shave, and then he would call her.

Freshly clothed, sitting on the apartment's small balcony, he sipped his coffee and made the call.

"Finn," she cried in welcome. "I was beginning to think I dreamed you up," she teased. Any sense of dread he had felt for taking so long to call was immediately wiped away.

"Hey, sorry I took so long."

"You're totally fine. The reason I left the message is twofold." Shit, he hadn't even checked his messages. She'd called?

"What are they?" he asked.

"One, I wanted us to visit Dasha. Then we can discuss my findings."

"What time?"

"Noon. Do you want to meet at my office first?"

"I'll meet you at the park." There was a long pause.

"Okay," she finally said.

"Did you want me to meet at your office?"

"No, the park is fine," she said brightly. Dammit, what was he missing? "I'll see you then." She cut the connection. Somehow he knew he had hurt her feelings. Well, he'd just have to fix it when he saw her.

Next, Finn dialed a familiar number. It was picked up on the first ring. He relaxed as soon as he heard his mother's voice.

"Hello, Mom."

"It's about damn time." Tears, love and righteous indignation. God, he loved Evie Crandall. The woman wouldn't put up with any man's shit, even her son's.

"Finn? Are you there?"

"I'm here, Mom," he assured her.

"Dammit, Finn. Come home. I thought you would be doing better if you went away for a little bit, but you don't sound better."

"I went out on a date," he said, trying to put some animation into his voice.

"You wouldn't lie to an old lady, now would you?" He listened to more than just her words, he listened to her voice. She was working hard to sound upbeat. He hated it.

"I don't know any old ladies to lie to."

"I'm fifty-two."

"Mom, you still have the guys in the grocery store hitting on you." He heard a small laugh. It made him feel good.

"Were you really out on a date?" she asked.

"We were talking about a case. It probably wasn't really a date."

"A case? What? Are you a lawyer? Tell me about the woman. Is she smart? Is she pretty? Is she good enough for you?" Ah, now that was the Evie Crandall he was used to.

"Mom, I'm trying to help this young girl. It's

complicated. I'm working with a private investigator. She's the one I went out with. It was just a one-time thing. We won't be going on a date again." Wasn't that a depressing thought? No more strawberry lip gloss for him.

"You won't see her again?" Evie asked.

"No, I'll see her. I'm seeing her today as a matter of fact. I just won't go on another date with her." Finn could practically hear his mother thinking.

"Finn honey, can I get a promise from you?"

"Is it important?"

"It is to me," she said with determination.

"I'll try, Mom."

"Don't hang up for five minutes. Give me five minutes. Okay, sweetie?" Fuck, this was going to be painful.

"All right."

"I've put some things together. I think I know where your head is at." God, he sure as hell hoped not.

"First, there was that bitch Ginger you dated while you were taking those college courses." Finn had to work hard not to crush the phone he was holding. "She made you think that it was your fault she lost the baby."

"You know the truth."

"Did I say you could talk yet?" Her voice was sharp. He shut up. "Dammit, Finn. She was drinking. How many times had you begged her to stop drinking while she was pregnant? It was her fault, not yours!"

"I should have been able to get her to stop–"

"She was a party girl. She had been looking for someone to sink her claws into, and force them to marry her. She got pregnant on purpose!"

He had never heard his Mom so vehement. Yeah, she had always told him that he wasn't to blame for Ginger losing the baby. But this was the first time she told him exactly how she felt about her.

"Mom, I get what you're saying. But that was still my son who died."

"And he was my grandson," Evie said quietly. "I mourn for him, and say prayers for him every single day. But I refuse to let my living son bury himself with him. Dammit, you did nothing wrong."

"Your time is almost up."

"Then there is your latest mission. I know it was bad because I have had every member of your team come over to my house. Hell, even Drake is walking on eggshells. But he's the easiest."

"What do you mean?" Drake damn well better have kept his mouth shut.

"I mean he's like a mother hen. He's so worried about you. He said you take too much to heart and that if there were such a thing as guilt pie, you would eat the whole thing. The man really understands you."

"I understand what I am, and am not, responsible for."

"No, you really don't, Finn. You've always thought you were responsible for the Western Hemisphere, and you're not. You need to be more like Declan. Now that boy will try to fix the Western Hemisphere, but he knows he's not responsible for it, and if it's fucked up, it wasn't his fault."

In his almost thirty years of life, he had never heard his mom drop the F-Bomb.

"So to sum things up Finn, because I've been keeping track of time, you are a good man. There has been some crap that has been shoved your way, but I need you to stop feeling like you were responsible for it. You weren't. You are a good man. You are a good man." Oh God, she was crying.

"Mom."

"I've got to go, honey. Please think about what I've said. I'm begging you."

"I will, Mom."

5

Finn strode across the grass towards the picnic benches. The others hadn't noticed his arrival, which amazed Angie. How could they not? Finn's presence was so formidable, she fantasized that the oak trees swayed toward him as he walked by.

"He's got your motor running, doesn't he girly?" her grandfather's tone was kind and loving.

"He does. But he has some demons he has to work through."

"I've seen it before," Pops agreed. She looked into his dark knowing eyes.

"What? What have you seen?"

"His kind of wounds." Then Finn was standing in front of her, and all of her attention was on him. He was wearing a black T-shirt and blue jeans. He gave a small tilt of his head, and she followed him away from the table.

"Is everything okay? Anything I need to know?" he asked.

"I wanted to run something past you. If my suspicions

are correct, we need to question Dasha because something is wrong."

She could tell she had his full attention. "Okay, what is it?"

"I hate how this sounds. But I hate even more that I'm probably right. This particular auction house they had going on in British Columbia was high-end, wasn't it?"

Finn thought back to the mansion and the endless stream of exotic sports cars. "Definitely."

"Then I think I might be right about what was going on up in Canada. I think the girls they used to breed weren't as attractive as the ones they sold as sex slaves. I went through the pictures, and there was a trend. I feel like a vicious bitch for noticing it. But I'm pretty sure I'm right."

Finn didn't flinch, she could see him mulling over what she said. "You're right."

"Except for Dasha. She's the one fly in the ointment." Angie said.

Finn's gaze flickered over to the girl sitting next to her uncle.

"Albert would have sold her to a client, not used her to breed." His face looked like it was carved from granite.

"Can you help me out a little?" Angie stroked her hand down his arm. His flinch was barely perceptible, but then he relaxed.

"What can I do?"

"Rylie's notes were really vague on how the girls were impregnated." She let her voice drift off.

"They were artificially inseminated. They were trying to produce specific types of babies, blue-eyed blondes, etc."

"So why would they have chosen to breed Dasha instead of selling her at the auction?" Angie asked.

"Oh God, she must have been raped, and gotten

pregnant," he answered quickly. Angie could see how the whole conversation ate at him. But it was important. She smoothed her hand along his arm until she could twine her fingers with his and squeezed. He looked into her eyes and she saw a moment of relief.

"I read Rylie's reports. Every one of those girls who was getting ready to be sold was given a birth control injection." His shoulders sagged. "Dasha must have been pregnant before the Liu's ever got ahold of her."

"So what are you saying?" he asked in a whisper, again glancing over at the girl.

"There is one more piece of information I got from Pops. It's not the US government Dasha is hiding from. She's trying to avoid anybody attached to the Ukrainian Embassy."

Finn tugged her hand. "Walk with me."

Holding this man's hand, and walking in one of her favorite places made this conversation easier. He let go of her hand, and before she could quell her disappointment, he put his arm around her shoulders and brought her in close to his body. She rested her head against his shoulder.

"You always smell like strawberries."

"I love strawberries. If there is a strawberry shampoo, lotion, or lip gloss, I use it." His fingers trailed along her shoulder.

"I'm beginning to love strawberries, too. I'm sorry I was M.I.A. Sometimes, I need time to get my head together."

"I think I understand."

He looked up into the trees that provided a lacy silhouette against the blue sky. "So Dasha was pregnant before she left the Ukraine. She probably fell for one of those 'Be a Model' or 'Be a Nanny' scams. She must be running from someone. Someone with clout with the Ukrainian government."

"Probably the father of her baby," Angie guessed.

"Probably."

"Hell, how do we get her to confide in us?" Angie blew out a frustrated breath making her hair fly up. He watched as it drifted back into place.

"If she hasn't told you so far, I'm not sure she's going to. Hell, she hasn't even told her uncle. Maybe I can get it out of her."

"I don't see how." She scowled.

"Unfortunately, working with less than cooperative witnesses is part of the job."

"It's mine too. Let me do this." Something told her that he didn't need any more scars on his soul.

"If my way doesn't work, you can bat clean-up." He rubbed a circle on her shoulder trying to soothe, trying to coax.

She turned and looked at him. "Seriously, let me try first."

"No." His tone brooked no argument. Looking at him, Angie had no doubt that one day he would be leading a whole contingent of men.

"Okay," she acquiesced.

THEY WALKED BACK to the picnic table, and Pops looked up from his chess game and grinned from ear-to-ear. It took Finn a split second to figure out what the hell was going on, then it dawned on him, the man thought that he and his granddaughter were an item. Dammit. He was going to have to set him straight, and quickly.

"Dasha, we need to talk." The girl looked fragile and worn sitting next to her big Ukrainian uncle.

"You have information?" Her eyes gleamed with interest.

"No. I *need* information. Who is Yulia's father?" Her eyes bulged.

"Hey. Wait just a damn minute–" Finn slashed his hand downwards, cutting off what Sergei was saying. The man went silent.

Dasha crossed her arms, trying to make herself look small, and shook her head.

"You haven't told us everything we need to know to save Yulia."

"I tell everything."

"No other girl was pregnant before she got to the Liu's. No other girl is trying to hide from her government. You need to tell us who Yulia's father is. You need to tell us why you are hiding."

"I cannot."

"You must." Her big eyes welled with tears.

"No. You cannot make me." She leaned into Sergei, who opened his mouth. Finn glared at the man, and he closed it.

"Dasha, if you want us to find Yulia... If you love your daughter. You will tell us the truth."

"I love my Yulia!"

She got up from the table and stumbled. She rushed around it until she stood in front of him. She grabbed his shirt.

"I sorry. I can't tell. If I tell, I die. Then Yulia has no mother. Please don't make me tell. Please. I beg you." Tears were falling wildly from her eyes. The anguish and pleading in her look sucked him in like a whirlpool. She grabbed both of his cheeks and stared into his eyes. "Please," she wailed.

Sweat broke out across his body, nausea roiled, and her features morphed into the girl from the farmhouse.

"No, no, God no," he choked out. He pulled her arms away from his face, and she fell backwards. Angie had grabbed her before she reached the ground. But Finn didn't see it, he was locked in another place, another time. He yanked his body away from the picnic bench and then fell onto the grass of the park. He wasn't seeing the trees above him, he was in the living room of the damned farmhouse, blue striped wallpaper, and a musty smell.

"Finn!"

He scrambled backwards on the wooden floor. This time, he was going to take out the other men before they had a chance to abuse the girls. He wasn't going to stand idly by and let the innocents be harmed on his watch again. He yanked up the cuff of his jeans and grabbed the knife from his boot.

"Finn, you're scaring me."

"Stay back, Angie," a man shouted. Finn turned on that voice. Was it Mike? He saw a man's shadow against the sun.

"You fucker. You won't get away with it this time." Finn was in a crouch, looking around for the others, before focusing in on his prey once again. "You'll die for what you've done to these girls."

"Finn, it's me, Angie."

A woman stepped up and put her arm around the man. "This is my grandfather. You're confused, Finn. This is my grandfather; he hasn't hurt anyone."

"He can't see us, Angie. We're in the sun." Finn shook his head. The man's voice wasn't familiar, and he sounded old. Why was the woman defending him?

"Finn, circle around so you can see us better," the woman's voice was soothing. It tickled a memory. "Please

Finn, you're in control. You have the weapon. Circle around so you can see us, okay?"

"Son, take a deep breath. Look around you. You're in a park in Austin, Texas. Smell the flowers." Again, it sounded like an old man talking. Finn shook his head to clear it. When he breathed in, he *did* smell flowers.

He kept his knife positioned in front of him and circled slowly around the man and woman until they came into focus. *The man wasn't Mike.*

"Finn, it's me, Angie. You're here in Austin, Texas. We're working to find Dasha's baby, remember?"

That was when he heard the sound of a girl whimpering.

"Stay put," he growled. He pivoted around and saw a young girl in the arms of another old man.

"Put down the knife, Finn, you're scaring her," the woman said.

"I don't understand." But he was beginning to. The girl crying was named Dasha. He remembered her. He turned back to Angie.

"Angie?" *What had he done?* He dropped the knife. Angie came over to him, and tried to put her arms around him, but he was having none of it. He stepped back.

"Stop." He made his voice a weapon as he picked up his knife, and carefully put it back into its sheath.

Lou Donatelli came over and looked him in the eye. "Looks to me like you've been through hell, son. No shame in that."

Finn knew better. He was a fucking liability.

He closed his eyes, then opened them. He looked over to where Dasha was in Sergei's arms. "Sir?" he asked. Sergei nodded. Finn went over to the two and crouched down in front of Dasha.

"What is wrong with you?" she asked, her teeth chattering.

He breathed out heavily. "Can you translate?" he asked Sergei. The man nodded again.

"I'm sick. Sometimes my mind plays tricks on me, and I think I am back in another place and another time. I helped to rescue some of the girls in Canada. It made me very sad and very mad while I was there. When you were upset with me, it reminded me of Canada, and I wanted to rescue you. I got confused and thought I was there again."

He waited while Sergei translated.

She nodded her head.

He wanted to continue questioning her. They needed answers, but he just couldn't manage it. He looked around him to see if Angie could ask the questions, but she wasn't there. Sergei and Dasha continued to talk in Ukrainian. Lou gave him an encouraging smile. He didn't even attempt to return it.

Finn stood to his full height and stretched. Damn, he had woken up that morning feeling full of hope.

6

As soon as he turned the corner, she could tell he noticed her waiting beside his car. His stride didn't change. He gave nothing away, but he'd noticed. She hurt for him, but she didn't intend to offer him any kind of sympathy, empathy, or succor. Nope, the man, had made it clear he didn't want any of the above.

"You're blocking my door."

"Observant. I admire that."

"Can you please move, ma'am." He did a remarkable Texas accent.

"I need a lift."

"I doubt it." He moved his hand toward the car door handle, but she wiggled her ass firmly against it. She looked up at him, daring him to reach for it.

"Angie, I really don't need these games now."

"I walked to the park. I need a ride back to the office. My feet are killing me." He looked down at her shoes and saw she was wearing heels.

"You know, for such a practical woman, you wear very impractical shoes."

She lifted her black patent leather pump. "But they make my legs look good." She watched him look at her legs. *Gotchya!*

"Fine, I'll drive you to the office."

"I told Sarah I'd pick up lunch."

"You're killing me," he said, as he went around and opened the passenger door for her. She waited patiently until he helped her slide into the seat. She'd be damned if they weren't going to return to normal as quickly as possible. If they didn't the man would probably go home and brood. Blow the whole incident out of proportion.

"I called in an order. It should be ready by the time we get there." He eyed her as he started the car.

"Where am I going?" She gave him directions and settled into the passenger making herself comfortable. When she tried to make conversation, he gave her monotone answers. She got the hint and turned on the radio.

She turned the dial until she managed to stop on one of her favorite songs. She couldn't help but notice that his fingers tapped twice to the beat. *Score!*

"Come inside with me. I won't be able to carry it all."

"How much did you order?" he asked as he followed her into the *taqueria*.

"Enough."

When he saw the three drinks, he stopped. "Dammit, Angie. I'm not having lunch with the two of you."

"Yes, you are. Do you want to have a fight here in the restaurant?" She switched to Spanish so the man handing over their lunch could enjoy the show.

Finn picked up the four sacks, three drinks, and headed outside.

"How many languages do you speak?" he asked.

"Three fluently, and I speak a little Italian. How about you?"

"Three. Spanish, English and Farsi." He put the sacks in the bed of the El Camino and she balanced the drinks on her lap. He drove to the office.

He parked the car. "Angie, stay where you are. I'll help you with the drinks." When they got into the elevator, he turned to her. "I'm not having lunch with you."

"I think you should."

"Really? After a guy pulls a knife on you, you think you should have lunch with him?" She laughed. She couldn't help it.

"Finn, we kissed after I pulled a gun on you. Get over your big bad self."

He was practically vibrating with frustration. "Hold these." She handed him the bags. His hands were now full with the drinks and the bags. She pressed the emergency stop on the elevator and looked at him. "Brace yourself."

"Ah fuck."

She walked behind him, pressed against him, wrapped her arms around his waist and rested her head between his shoulder blades.

"It's okay to be human." He was so stiff, she felt wave after wave of hurt emanating off of him. He would never admit it. So she just held him, hoping some of what she was feeling would get through to him.

What are you feeling, Angela Jo?

She sighed against him. Even after everything that had happened at the park, Finn made her feel safe. This was a man who would lay down his life for those in need. This was a man who felt so deeply, he was scarred because of his deep feelings. Yes, she felt safe. She was beginning to feel so much more. It scared her because she didn't think he was anywhere near ready to reciprocate her feelings.

———

THE ALARM GOING off in the elevator was jarring, but years of training kept him from moving a muscle. Angie brushed a kiss into the middle of his back, and then she slid around him, she kept one hand on him the entire time. She used the other to press the emergency button to get the elevator moving again.

"I could eat," his voice was husky. God, the woman, had a way about her.

"Good, I bought enough to feed an army."

"Let's hope you bought enough to feed the Navy," he said as he followed her down the hallway to her office. Sarah was waiting for them.

"It's about time. I thought I might actually end up losing a pound today. We wouldn't want that to happen." She took the drinks and bags from Finn and headed towards the conference room.

The two women were like a well-oiled machine. It was clear they'd had this food for lunch before.

"Finn, you have to try this salsa, it's to die for." He really looked at Sarah for the first time. She was a little older than his mother but had that same air of competence. It was nice to see that Angie surrounded herself with people like that. It said something about her.

"How hot is it?"

"Oh, it's hot," Sarah said, her eyes twinkling. "But you're a big boy, I figure you can handle it." She scooped up another mouthful with her tortilla chip and took a bite. He watched her chew and then wave her hand in front of her mouth. He immediately broke into a cold sweat. He blinked rapidly.

You're in Austin. Sarah's fine, Crandall. She's eating tortilla chips. Breathe.

"Come on, don't you want to try some?" She pushed the cup of salsa towards him. He eyed the dip warily. Could he do this? His hand trembled slightly. He *could* do this. It wasn't like the park. He wasn't being taken by surprise.

He scooped up a bite with a chip and thought his head might explode. Both women laughed as he took the lid off his sweet tea and took a couple of long gulps of the drink. He felt a sense of euphoria that he had gotten through the moment, even if he was a pansy and needed to drink a gallon of tea.

"Wait a moment. Sarah, I think we need to take a picture. I'm pretty sure it was a smile I just saw on Finn's face."

He shook his head at Angie's antics.

"Oops, it's too late. Like the mythical bigfoot. You snooze, you lose."

"So tell me about Dasha," Sarah asked. "Do you think you're any closer to finding her baby?"

"There are some interesting developments in her case," Angie said.

"Okay, I know when I'm being stonewalled." Sarah smiled.

"It's not that," Angie protested. "We'll just know more tomorrow. You are coming back tomorrow?" she asked hesitantly.

"Yes, I'll be here." She relaxed, and he realized it was a big deal for her. Even though he'd only known her for a week, he didn't intend to be one more person that abandoned her.

"I'm impressed by what you figured out. I know our team never picked up on the fact that there was a difference in the girls who were being sent to the island for breeding."

Angie flushed. "I'm not proud of noticing."

"Why?"

"I feel crappy for basically saying 'you're cute' and 'you're not'."

"Angie, you got into the heads of the Liu's. That was exactly what you wanted to do. You weren't judging the girls yourself." He watched as she gave a tentative smile.

"Let me get this straight, you're kicking yourself because you noticed that some of the girls were more attractive than some of the others?" Sarah asked.

When Angie didn't answer, Finn nodded.

"Don't make me slap you. You're supposed to notice things. Just because you don't want to judge a book by its cover, doesn't mean you're supposed to put your head in the sand. I swear sometimes you're too damn nice for this job. Thank God you no longer believe every sob story that comes into this office."

"Sarah, no telling tales."

"She used to take so many pro bono cases, that for the first year I thought we would go out of business."

"I did not."

"How about the woman who ended up inheriting seven million dollars from her husband's estate, and never paid you a dime?" Sarah demanded.

"You have to admit, after that, I learned my lesson."

"It was a damn hard lesson to learn." Sarah turned to Finn. "I'm now in charge of the billing. I limit her to three pro bono cases a year. Dasha is the fourth." Sarah picked up another chip and waved it at him. "It's only August. Apparently, I'm not doing my job well."

"She's pretty tough to manage, isn't she?" Finn asked.

"Yes, she is. Now eat up. It looks like you're not up to your fighting weight."

Finn eyed the older woman. How did she know?

"I have three sons. I know when a boy has lost weight."

"I'm hardly a boy."

"Have you turned thirty yet?" Sarah asked as she bit into her food.

"No."

She pressed a napkin against her lips. "Then you're a boy. Now eat up. We ordered double for you."

Finn could have eaten triple. The food was great.

"Don't worry, I have homemade pecan pie for dessert. You won't starve," Sarah said as she read his mind.

"How old are your sons?" Finn asked.

"Thirty-two, twenty-eight, and thirteen." Finn had to take another big gulp of his drink.

"Yep, it's always the thirteen-year-old that takes people by surprise. Took me by surprise as well. Harry retired last year. He loves being a stay-at-home dad. I'll bring in the pie."

He turned to Angie. "Thank you for forcing me to come to lunch. I probably would have just gone to the apartment and obsessed."

"I heard what you said to Dasha. I read the reports. I'm amazed you're doing as well as you are."

"I don't need anyone to blow smoke up my ass," he said in a hard voice. He could do without the pie. Angie put her hand on his arm.

"Finn, I'm not. I have a cousin Bruno. He came home from Iraq five years ago. He wasn't injured on the outside. But it took three years and some intensive counseling before he recovered. My aunt and uncle were frantic. Now he's married with a baby on the way, but he still struggles. So I would say that you're doing remarkably well."

Finn rubbed the back of his neck and then stopped. It was what Mason did when he was uncomfortable, and he hated doing something that people might recognize as a sign of discomfort.

"Look, it's different for me. Your cousin was probably a volunteer. I've trained for this all of my adult life."

"What a load of bullshit. What's more, you're now putting down every other person who struggles with PTSD. Basically saying they're weak. Is that really what you want to say?"

"God no!" He was stunned that she would even think that.

"Then you're going to have to learn to give yourself some of the same slack as you would others in your shoes. Now, we have a case to discuss." Finn watched as she pulled out her purse, grabbed her lip gloss and a compact and reapplied. He couldn't decide what had gotten him more hot and bothered, the smell of strawberries, or the fact that she had just managed to effectively call him on his bullshit.

FINN WAS PUTTING AWAY his groceries when the phone rang. It was Angie's number, and he answered the phone.

"Hello."

"Hey, Finn." Angie's voice was kind of muffled.

"Are you at the office? Do you want me to swing by and pick you up?" He figured he could get a run in before their meeting.

"I'm not. I need to cancel. Do you mind talking to Dasha

by yourself today?" He was having trouble understanding her.

"Are you all right?" He heard her swallow.

"I'm fine," she enunciated carefully.

"Why are you talking funny?"

"It's a long story. After you talk to Dasha, can you give me a call?"

"Why aren't you going with me?" He heard her take a deep breath. It almost sounded like she was wheezing. "Dammit Angie, you don't sound well."

"I'm fine. Just talk to Dasha. You know it's important."

"You're important too. Where are you?"

"I'm at home. I'm not feeling well."

"So you're sick. Instead of calling you after I talk to Dasha, I'll come over."

"No!" she cried out. He heard a little hiss. Oh fuck, she was hurting. Clammy hands clutched his throat.

"I'll be over in a few minutes." He hung up and grabbed his keys with trembling fingers. His phone started ringing again. He saw it was Angie, and he ignored it.

It was a twenty-minute drive to her house. He made it in fifteen.

Before he could knock, she opened the door. It was sweltering outside, but the woman was bundled up to her neck in sweats. Her hair was falling over her face. He could barely see her.

"I'm contagious. You need to leave."

His eyes zeroed in on her swollen lip. He took a deep breath.

You can do this, Crandall.

He pushed open the door gently when his instinct was to push his way inside so he could get to her, hold her, make sure she was okay.

"I'm coming in, Angie." He made sure his tone was firm but gentle.

"I don't feel well," she said in the petulant voice of a child.

"I don't imagine you do," he said as he stepped into the foyer and got his first really good look at her. He carefully brushed back the curls from her face and tilted her chin so he could see her face more clearly. "Ahh, lady. Somebody really did a number on you."

How in the hell could tenderness and rage be fighting for dominance in his mind and body at the same time?

"I'm really fine," but her voice trembled the slightest bit, and one of her puffy eyes held the sheen of tears.

Tenderness first. "Have you been icing?"

"I just woke up."

"Dammit. You did go to the hospital, didn't you?" She winced at his words. "Sorry. Tenderness." His fingers sifted through the silk of her hair and found a good sized goose-egg. "Tell me you went to the hospital. You could have a concussion. Tell me you didn't come home and go to sleep."

She shrugged away from him. "Fine, I won't tell you," she said angrily.

She took two steps, and he saw she was limping and holding her side. He might lose it. But he'd be damned if it was going to happen two days in a row. And it *sure* as hell wasn't going to be when Angie needed him.

He bent, put one arm under her knees, the other behind her back, and lifted her high and strode to the couch in her living room.

"Finn! Put me down!" she shrieked.

"Fine." He settled her onto the sofa. She huffed out a moan. He wanted to know everything, but first things were first.

"Do I need to call an ambulance?"

"Of course not!" she said indignantly.

"Well since you don't seem to have the sense God gave a gnat, it's a reasonable question. Do you think your ribs are broken, cracked, or bruised?"

"How'd you know there was anything wrong with my ribs?"

"Angie, answer the question," he commanded.

She looked at him with wide eyes. "I'm pretty sure just bruised. But what does it matter, if they're cracked they just tape them anyway."

Calm down, Crandall. Do not channel Drake. Do not talk like Drake would talk.

He tried to lift the hem of her sweatshirt, but she slapped at his hands. He glowered, and she stopped. He lifted the shirt to the bottom of her breasts. She wasn't wearing a bra, but that didn't capture his attention. It was the two clear boot prints that sent his blood pressure skyrocketing.

Before they got to the who, he needed to know what else was wrong. She coughed and wheezed. Goddammit, her lungs did not sound good. She winced and held her head.

"Where else were you kicked?"

"Nowhere."

"You were limping." He smoothed her shirt back down and cupped her cheek. "I'm holding onto my temper by a thread. Do you really want to lie to me at this point?" He could see her assessing him.

"He kicked my hip and my knee."

"How bad?"

"The knee not so bad," she admitted.

Finn laid his hand down on her right hip, the side he

had seen her favor. It was hot to the touch even through the crimson sweats. "I'm going to look."

"I know," she said quietly.

He tugged down the pants, revealing her hip, while still preserving her modesty. The bruise was a deep purple. It amazed him she had been able to walk.

"We're getting some ice. Then I'm taking you to the hospital. In the car, you can tell me what in the hell happened."

She tried to push away from him, but he easily and gently held her down. She finally settled and stared up at him.

"Look, Finn, I am not going to the hospital. If I felt I needed to go to the hospital, I would have gone last night when the EMT's tried to take me," she said reasonably.

He froze. "Let me get this right. EMT's evaluated you, and determined you should go to the hospital, and you refused care?" he asked slowly.

"Yes! Now you can see why I'm not going to go now."

"Oh lady, you're going." He didn't care how much venom she spit. "You're going. You are going to do exactly what every medical professional tells you to do. You are going to come home and follow every order they give you even if I have to stay here to get you to do it. Then when you get well, I'm going to–" he stopped before he said spank her ass. That was the old Finn. He would never say that to a woman again, not after all the violence he had seen heaped on them. But he had to admit his damn palm was itching. What the hell had she been thinking?

"Oh for God's sake." She pushed up again and then gasped.

"Ribs, hip, or head?"

"Ribs," she replied. "Okay, I'll go. But only because I

think it might not hurt to have my ribs X-Rayed, not because you're bullying me." She folded her arms and gasped in pain. Finn flinched.

He stood up and found a hell of a lot of ice packs in the freezer. Far more than any normal person should have. Two of them were the type that would wrap around an arm or a leg with Velcro, and should work on her knee.

"Do you have first aid tape?" he asked as he brought the ice packs back to the living room. At her blank expression, he rephrased the question. "Do you have medical wrap, so I can keep the ice packs in place?"

"There's a first aid kit in the master bathroom." She waved towards the hallway. He found the kit, and as he worked to get the ice packs in place, he continued to ask her questions.

"Tell me how this happened. I assume you were working a case."

"It doesn't matter, I held my own and the asshole that did this is in jail."

"Who was he? Are you trying to tell me this was random?"

"No, it wasn't random. His name is Paul Jackson, and he's pissed because I took his wife's case."

"Tell me about it."

"Lorna has a restraining order against him, but he works in the mayor's office, and filed one against her too. He's making her out to look crazy. Therefore, the Austin Police haven't been as quick as they should to show up at her apartment when she calls."

"Damn. That sounds ugly."

"It's worse than that. He's been escalating, and she can't get anyone to believe her."

"Except for you, right?"

"Right."

"Why did he attack you? How did he know you were working for Lorna?"

"She told him I was her bodyguard. She'd had him served with divorce papers at his office yesterday. We knew he was going to lose his shit and go over to her apartment, so I was going to be at her place after he received the papers. Unfortunately, I underestimated him."

"What do you mean?"

"He attacked me in Lorna's parking garage as soon as I got out of my car."

"Tell me exactly what happened."

"I left my office at three and headed straight to Lorna's place. He jumped me in the causeway between the apartment complex and the parking garage. He hit me in the head before I could do anything, then he pulled a gun on me and dragged me behind the dumpsters." She swallowed and clutched at her throat. He touched her hand, trying to keep both of them in the present. It wasn't enough. He sat beside her on the couch and hauled her onto his lap. He didn't want to hear this, but she needed to talk, and he needed to be there for her, and keep it together.

Angie looked at him in surprise, and then he coaxed her head to rest on his chest. She snuggled against him, with a trembling sigh.

"It's okay, Angie. I'm here. Keep going."

"My head hurt, and he was pulling my hair. He was waving the gun, the dumb son of a bitch. I hit him hard in the shoulder, and the gun went flying. But he's a big guy, really big. He punched me, and I fell to the ground. I screamed, but he didn't care. He said he was going to kill me, and nobody would ever guess it was him."

Finn felt bile rise.

"He started toward me, but I kicked his ankle. That's when he started to kick me."

Angie trembled at the memory, and Finn gently rocked her in his arms. She burrowed deeper. It was clear both of them were comforted by their connection. "I finally was able to roll away and get my gun out of my purse. As soon as I had it in my hands, he went down to his knees with his hands up. I just couldn't bring myself to shoot him, even though I wanted to, Finn. I really did."

"Of course, you did. Don't feel bad for wanting to hurt or kill that bastard." Finn wanted to get his hands on the man. Just two minutes should do the job.

"Somebody must have called 911 when I was screaming because the cops showed up almost at the same time."

"Wait a minute." He tipped her chin so he could look at her. "The cops didn't insist you go to the hospital?"

"I signed a refusal of care form. And they couldn't force me to go to the hospital."

Finn kept one arm around Angie, holding her carefully against him. He pulled out his phone and called her office.

"Sarah? This is Finn. Angie was badly beaten last night. She refused to go to the hospital. If you can tell me which hospital I should take her to, I'll go there, and you can tell her grandfather to meet us there."

"You bastard," Angie screeched. She wiggled to get away from him, but it was useless. He was careful not to hurt her, but he sure as hell wasn't going to let her go. Finn listened while Sarah agreed and gave him the information he needed. He loved how she didn't ask any unnecessary questions, just said she would be shutting down the office and would meet them there.

Finn put his phone in his pocket and looked down at

Angie. Now that he had her where he wanted her, and he had a plan, he relaxed. It was time to let loose.

"Let me get this straight. You were going to go over to your client's house, and she has a batshit, crazy husband. You were going to go over there alone when you had a Navy SEAL you could take along. Do I understand that correctly?"

"He'd never used a gun before," Angie said belligerently.

"You knew you're dealing with some fucking psycho who you admitted had been escalating. You do know domestic abuse cases are the ones most apt to result in violence, or don't you?"

"Of course, I do," she said defensively.

"Then what the fuck were you thinking?" he asked in an ominous tone.

"That I could handle this. I've handled other cases just fine."

"I'm sure you have. Bravo. When did you decide not to use all of the resources at your disposal? Do you think you're a goddamn superhero?"

Fuck, that definitely sounded like Drake.

"Back off. You have no right."

"I have every right. We're working a case together. Less than a week ago we were considering sleeping together. I have all the rights in the world to be concerned for your safety. I, I..."

She gave him a long considering look. "You what, Finn?"

"I can't handle the idea of you getting hurt when I could have been there to help you. I just can't." He pressed his forehead against hers. Their eyes met, he could see her bruised flesh, but mostly just the warmth and intelligence of Angie.

"I'm sorry, I guess I wasn't thinking."

He felt something in him ease.

"Good, from now on it will occur to you to call me."

She cupped his cheek.

"I'm so sorry. If I'm honest, there was a moment when I considered calling you, but we're only working the Dasha case, so I figured I'd handle this one on my own."

He reared back. "God-Mother-Fucking-Dammit Donatelli! You are so going over my knee as soon as you are recovered. You thought about calling me, and you didn't?! Are you out of your ever loving mind? Do you have no concept of team? You let your teammates cover your six. You never go in alone. Not when a teammate is available! Never!"

Her brown eyes were huge. She didn't look scared. She was looking at him in shock.

"Maybe you're right."

"Repeat after me. Finn Crandall is abso-fucking-lutely right."

"But..."

His palm itched again. Is this how Drake always felt? He didn't feel anything but righteous anger, and a cleansing sense of relief that he was telling Angie exactly what he thought, as he thought it. Maybe Drake was onto something.

"Repeat it."

"Finn Crandall is right, *just* about this."

He stood up with her in his arms. "We're going to the hospital now."

"I'm feeling kind of queasy. I'm hot. Can you get me a 7-Up?" He looked at her and saw she was looking a little green around the gills. He turned and settled her back onto the sofa and went to the kitchen. There was only Sprite. He brought it back to her.

"Thanks, this will hit the spot."

"You asked for a 7-Up."

"I know."

"This is a Sprite."

"Don't get all persnickety." He opened the bottle, and she took a long gulp and sighed in pleasure.

He carefully lifted her up and took her to the front door. "Set the alarm. The asshole is probably out on bail by now, and knows where you live."

She looked at him with wide eyes. "I don't think so. It was a violent attack."

"Don't underestimate the fact that he has ties to the mayor's office." Finn sighed. He wished it was fucking different. But it wasn't.

"Damn, you're right. I wasn't thinking." He got her into his car and fastened her seatbelt. He got to the hospital fast and pulled up to the entrance. Sarah was already waiting beside an orderly with a wheelchair. God love the woman. Finn stopped the car, ran to the passenger side, swung Angie into his arms, and settled her into the chair.

"Her grandfather should be here any time." Sarah squatted beside Angie and looked at her with tears in her eyes.

They all looked up as a Bentley damn near crashed into the back of Finn's El Camino.

"What the fuck?"

"Pops," the two women said in unison. Lou Donatelli scrambled out of the expensive vehicle and rushed over to his granddaughter. "Not again."

Again?

"Pops, we need to get her inside," Sarah said as she started to push the chair.

"Let me," Finn said as he put his hand on one of the handles. Sarah nodded. Lou and Sarah walked beside the chair. Lou held onto Angie's hand as they made their way to the front desk to sign in.

"Finn, talk to me. What the fuck happened?" Finn watched as the two women talked to the nurse at the front desk. Sarah was really upset, but holding it together.

Finn explained everything Angie had told him. "Dammit. This is the worst I've ever seen her."

"How often does this happen?" Finn asked.

"The last time was two years ago. That bastard is still in jail," Lou assured him. "At least, this time, she shouldn't end up with any scars."

Scars?

"She told me that most of your clientele was corporate."

"It is. But she keeps taking these pro bono cases where someone is in trouble. Those are the ones where she ends up in hurt. It sounds like this one isn't over yet."

7

"Finn, we need to talk to Dasha today. They kept me in here far too long."

"You had a concussion, and were throwing up," Sarah said in too high of a voice. "Of course, they kept you for three days. They needed to make sure you were all right before releasing you. We were all worried."

"Well, I'm fine. I caught a bug in the hospital. The doctors said so," Angie huffed. "Now we need to focus on Dasha."

"Angie, settle down and listen to me." Her grandfather put his hand on hers. She looked up at him from the hospital chair.

"Pops, I know you want to talk about the Jackson's, but we need to work on Dasha's case. I'm getting out of the hospital today, and finding Yulia is the most important thing."

"No, it's not! Now you listen to me, young lady. I was at court. They're going to let him out on bail until the trial. He acted like such a pillar of the community. It made me sick," Pops said.

"We knew he was going to do that. It's behind us. Now we have to look forward. It's been too long since we followed up with her."

"Listen to your grandfather," Sarah said, from where she was sitting on the hospital bed. "I know you don't want to think about Paul Jackson, but this isn't going away."

Angie shuddered. She still remembered Paul's shoe kicking her in the ribs.

"Sarah's right. He caught up with Lorna and me in the hallway at the courthouse after the hearing. He said he wasn't done with her or 'that bitch.' His lawyer pulled him away before he could say more."

Angie glanced at Finn, who was standing against the wall near the door. He had been there during every visiting hour since she had been in the hospital. He didn't say anything as her grandfather explained what had been said, but he'd looked colder with every word her grandfather uttered.

"Dammit," Sarah gasped. "We've got to do something. Angie, we can't let him hurt you again."

"I don't care about me," Angie protested. "We have to protect Lorna."

"Lorna quit her job. She was planning on packing when I left her."

"Pops," Angie wailed. "She can't do that. She can't let him win."

"She said she'd be back for the trial, but she just can't take it right now. Personally, I think she's being smart." Angie looked at her grandfather and silently admitted he might be right. "I'm worried about you," he said.

"Now that I know to be on the lookout, I'll be fine."

"Not good enough," Pops declared.

"I agree," Sarah seconded.

"He has too many connections. He'll be able to find out where you live," Pops warned her. Angie had to work hard to keep showing a strong front. She knew she'd have to stay alert. Paul Jackson was going to be a problem.

"I have a great security system, Pops."

"You'll stay with me at the ranch," her grandfather growled.

"I will not. Hell, you're practically a celebrity, everybody knows you. I'm not putting you in danger."

"You can stay with me. Nobody knows about me," Sarah said.

Angie and Pops said "No," at the same time.

"You'll stay with me," Finn said quietly.

Angie covered her face. *Fuck.*

"Perfect. It's settled." Could Pops have responded any faster?

"I agree," Sarah said, jumping in with both feet.

"You are traitors—both of you." Angie looked at Finn. His expression hadn't changed since Pops explained the situation. He looked like a Viking warrior who must be one of his ancestors.

"Finn, you don't really want me underfoot," she tried to reason.

"You're staying with me." He didn't try to cajole, wasn't commanding, he was just telling her the sky was blue.

"Dammit, Finn. You can't tell me what to do."

"He got you to the hospital, didn't he?" Sarah reminded her. "And it was a damn good thing since one of your ribs was broken. Sometimes you don't have any sense."

"It wasn't a big deal, they just taped it, you're making a mountain out of a molehill."

"They had to realign it, so it didn't puncture your lung," Sarah persisted.

Angie couldn't decide between sticking out her tongue or flipping her the bird, so she didn't do anything.

Sarah turned to Finn and Pops. "Okay gentlemen, you need to leave while I help Angie dress." As soon as the men left, Angie turned on Sarah.

"I can't stay with him."

"Give me one good reason why you can't."

"I'm beginning to really like the man."

"So what's the problem?"

"I refuse to put myself in a situation where I'm next to a man, day in and day out, where I'm falling in like, and I don't know where he stands. It'll be too awkward."

"Or it could be a great opportunity. Here are your clothes." Sarah put some loose pants and a long white tunic on the bed. "The top is fleece. I didn't figure you would want to wear a bra."

"Sarah, this is too embarrassing. I want my own space."

"Well, it's not in the cards right now. Anyway, you need to work on the missing baby case, and this allows you to while still keeping you protected."

"Sarah–"

"Enough. This is a closed subject. Now let's get you into the wheelchair so you can get the hell out of the hospital. You know you want out."

"Yes," Angie admitted.

Sarah pushed her into the hall, and the men were waiting for them.

Angie tried one last time. "I could stay at a hotel."

"Do you want to explain why that would be preferable to staying with me?" Finn asked in a reasonable tone of voice.

"Yes, I'd like to hear this," Pops said. "Especially since you're hurt and he can protect you. I think this would be interesting."

She looked at the three people surrounding her. She sighed. "You're absolutely right. Finn, thanks for offering. I appreciate being able to stay at your apartment."

"It's no problem."

FINN BREATHED his first calm breath since he had seen Angie beaten up. Having her in his apartment, under his watch, soothed him. When Declan first gave him the keys to the two-bedroom apartment, he had thought it was too big, now he was glad to have it. Sleeping on the couch really didn't have a lot of appeal, but he had certainly slept in worse places.

"I called Dasha. She and Sergei will be over later this afternoon."

The woman wouldn't know the word 'quit' if it bit her in the ass. He was damn tempted to call up Sergei and postpone the meet until tomorrow.

He had her settled on his couch, with pillows propped up behind her. "I'll allow it, as long as you eat and nap."

"What the hell do you mean, 'you'll allow it?'" She pushed herself up and winced. "Who died and made you the boss of me?"

Finn rubbed both hands through his short cropped hair. "I'm not the boss of you. But since I'm the only one in this place in tune with your pain and stamina levels, I guess I'm putting myself in charge. Look at yourself. You damn near keeled over by the time we made it up the stairs." He was still kicking himself for listening to her instead of carrying her like he'd wanted.

"Having a conversation with someone is not taxing."

He decided to try another tactic. He crouched beside

her. "Angie, you and I both know this is going to be a tough conversation. Dasha finally promised to tell us what in the hell is going on. We'll have to wade through a lot of bullshit. This is going to be complicated, and you need to be at your best. We both do."

She looked at him for a long time, considering his words. "What do you have to eat?"

"Ah, the Pre-Law brain is finally functioning." He gave her a relieved look. "Would you like an omelet?"

"That sounds great. Do you have meat to put in it?"

"Ham?"

"Perfect. I was worried that since you're from California, it would be nothing but vegetables." She gave him a cheeky grin.

"Brat."

When he brought back the food, her eyes were at half-mast. "Angie?" She straightened up.

"Milk?"

"You need your strength. I'm drinking it too." He held up his glass, and she smiled.

"Thanks." She started to eat. He waited until she began to pick up steam, clearly getting a little more energy.

"Why didn't you want to stay with me?"

"What?" she asked as her fork was midway to her mouth.

"I asked, why you didn't want to stay with me."

She set down her fork and pressed the paper towel to her lips. "I didn't want to be a burden."

He snorted. "Want to try again? Maybe the truth this time?"

"Look, we don't even know one another. We went on one sort-of date. You're only in town as long as it takes to find Dasha's baby. Volunteering to watch out for me is ridiculous." He loved seeing the flash of fire in her brown eyes.

"You have to admit it makes sense."

"I don't have to admit shit." She set the plate on the coffee table. "I'm not hungry anymore."

"You've barely eaten a third of your food."

"I'm tired, I'm going to take a nap." She leaned back and shut her eyes. Finn was beyond frustrated, mostly with himself. He shouldn't have pushed her. She needed to eat.

But at least he had the answers he wanted. It came down to their one 'sort-of date,' and that he would leave after Dasha's case was over. He was pretty sure that Angie was beginning to have feelings for him. He wasn't sure if it was a good thing or a bad thing. The woman was on his mind way too fucking much. Her strength, her kindness, her humor, her resilience. It had been easier when he thought the feelings were just on his side, to think she might be thinking about him as well made this much tougher...and easier.

"Finn?" She was lying there with her eyes closed.

"Yes."

"I can feel you looking at me. Go away."

"Why? You're not sleeping."

"I can't sleep with you staring at me."

"Angie, can you look at me?"

"Don' wanna." Damn, he forgot she'd taken a pain tablet. Still, they needed to get this out in the open.

"Just for a second. Please?" She opened one eye, then both.

"Fine," she huffed out.

"I don't know if you're ready to hear this, but here goes nothing." He saw he had her full attention. "I care for you." Her eyes widened.

"You do not."

He cupped her cheek and let his thumb graze over her lip. "Yes. Yes, I do. Am I in this by myself?"

She nuzzled against his hand and sighed.

"No. No, you're not in this alone. But I'm scared, Finn."

"We'll go slow, okay?" She looked at him with eyes that were beginning to heat with desire.

"How slow?"

"I'm going to kiss you. All right?"

"Yes please."

He cupped her head with his right hand and brushed his lips against hers. No strawberries this time, just Angie. Perfect. Slowly, because she was injured. Slowly, because she had just been abused at the hands of a man and he wanted to erase the terror. Slowly, because he wanted to savor this feeling. He parted his lips and reveled as hers followed. He sipped and licked her plump bottom lip, enjoying her sigh of satisfaction.

She curled her arms around his head, trying to force him closer. But this was going to be at his pace. Her curls seemed to be alive under his fingers, so soft, silky, and springy to the touch. She broke away, he pulled back, despite the fact she was trying to pull him to her.

"Harder," she demanded. His heart softened at her request.

"Gentle," he whispered, and dipped down for more.

He kissed the dimple on her cheek, and then stroked it with his tongue, her groan shot straight to his cock. He nipped kisses all the way along her jaw, then back to her mouth as she panted his name.

"I'm here."

This time, he thrust his tongue deep, and she sucked him in. Her mouth was a warm cavern that made his body harden and his mind swirl. In and out, he explored and dominated this woman who was taking everything he had to give. She groaned again as she tried to pull him closer. Even through his haze of want, he was cognizant of her injuries. He didn't press down but reasoned that stroking was allowed.

He rested his elbow beside her and brushed his knuckles down the side of her left breast. When she jerked and gasped, he stopped. He pulled away from the kiss and looked into her dazed brown eyes.

"Angie?"

"Again."

"No. You have to stay still." He heard the hint of pain in her voice.

"Are you kidding me?"

"No, I'm not," his voice implacable. Her eyes began to focus, and she licked the moisture from her slick lips. It was his turn to groan. "Honey, please, for me. I can't stand to see you in pain, but I have to touch you."

"I promise not to move if you help me out of my top." He froze.

"I need your hands on my naked skin. If you do that, I promise not to move. Please, Finn. Please."

God, he wanted it so badly. Nothing had ever felt so clean and good. He didn't *just* want this—he *needed* this. He moved so his hand cradled her back, and carefully lifted her off the pillows so she was sitting up.

"Are you sure?"

"More than anything."

He raised her tunic and helped her slide it off her arms, and then pull it over her head. He sucked in his breath. There were bandages around her middle, and below that, a rainbow of bruising, but above were her unmarred breasts, topped with beautiful pink and brown nipples.

Mouthwatering. He had trouble looking away from the bounty before him.

"Finn?"

He immediately looked up and saw she was apprehensive. "Lady, you're beautiful."

"I'm a bruised mess, but I need you to touch me." She bit her bottom lip. "That is if you want to."

His heart ached for her. He got the feeling she wasn't normally unsure of her appeal, but this trauma had made her hesitant.

"Oh Angie, I'm dying here." He clasped her small hand in his big one and guided it to the front of his jeans. "Don't doubt for one moment that I want you."

Her eyes turned drowsy, and she cupped and caressed him through the thick denim.

"Oh no. We're not going to start something we can't finish."

"Why can't we finish it?" She pouted.

"Because you're not up to big girl play. Right now we're going to stick to the minor leagues." He wrapped his arms around her and bent his head. He couldn't wait a second longer. He lapped his tongue around the bud of her nipple, savoring the taste and texture of the beautiful woman in his arms.

Angie cried out but didn't move because he had her gently but firmly wrapped in his arms. "So good." She was right. He laved, and then suckled the firm flesh, delighting in the way her skin heated. She gripped his short hair, pulling hard.

Finn licked his way upwards and kissed the mouth that was crying out so passionately. If she kept it up, there was no way he wouldn't take this to the next level, and the next, and the next. Slowly, he stroked her back, careful of her injuries, settling down their out of control passion. This time, he simply kissed her dimple, then rested his forehead against hers, and they stared into each other's eyes.

"I want more, Finn," Angie's voice a breathless quiver.

"So do I, lady, so do I."

"Why did you stop?"

"You know why."

She blew out a sigh. "Yes. But don't think my injuries are going to save you next time Mr. Big Bad SEAL." Finn let out a startled laugh.

"Gotchya. You smiled and laughed," Angie said in a delighted tone. "Why don't you do that more often?"

"Because you haven't been almost naked in my arms before?"

"I don't think that's the reason, but I'll let you get away with it for now." She stroked her hand down his cheek. "When you're ready to talk, I'll be here for you." He gripped her hand and kissed her palm.

"I appreciate it."

"Now help me dress. Dasha and Sergei will be here soon."

THE MAN MADE her melt all over the place. He was almost twice the size of Dasha, and he managed to make her feel comfortable. Angie was propped up on the couch, and he had moved the ottoman next to her to sit on. It was a smart move because it made him sit lower. Then he had Sergei and Dasha sit together on the loveseat.

"Dasha told me everything last night. She wanted to practice before telling you," Sergei explained. "We're in trouble."

"My baby? Do you know more about my baby?" Dasha asked leaning forward hopefully.

"I'm sorry, honey. We don't." The girl slumped against her uncle.

"Can I get you something to drink?" Finn asked them.

Dasha shook her head. She was gripping her uncle's hand tightly. She took a deep breath and expelled it. "I love my Uri much, much. He young, but have power." She looked at Sergei, who nodded. "He with Bratva. I not know."

"Fuck," Finn muttered.

"What's Bratva?" Angie asked.

"The Russian mob."

"Ukrainian mob, too," Sergei answered. "What the hell, the same thing. But the mob is mixed up with the government. They go hand in hand."

Dasha's eyes filled with tears. "I know Uri for two years. He will to marry me. He promised. I am so happy because I am to have baby."

Sergei bent his head and said something in Ukrainian, and Dasha wiped her eyes and nodded. "Then Uri meet me his boss. His boss is General." Dasha leaned forward and looked first at Finn, then at Angie. "This man. This man is much evil. He tell Uri he will pay for me."

"Uri laughed, he think it is how you say? Joke." Dasha pointed at Angie. "Uri tell about baby. General no care. We have three days because General must leave town. When he come back, I must go to him."

"What did you do?" Angie asked.

"Uri do." She turned to her uncle and spoke quickly in Ukrainian. He sighed, and turned to Finn and Angie.

"Uri's family dealt in diamonds. Dasha's not sure exactly what he did. She just knows that he often had bags of cash, and he would exchange them for diamonds and return those to the General. There's a lot of illegal arms selling going on in the Ukrainian army. It's my guess that's what was going on. It gets worse. Tell them, sweetheart."

"Uri put diamonds in train station locker. We to use for to get away. He put papers in locker too. He say it is." She said a word in Ukrainian.

Sergei translated. "Insurance. I'm sure he has the general by the shorthairs."

"Great, we can get the diamonds and papers and end this!" Angie said excitedly.

Dasha shook her head sadly. "I not know which locker. I forget."

"Shit," Finn said dejectedly.

"Dasha, do you know what was on the papers?" Angie asked as she leaned forward.

Dasha turned towards her uncle, who translated. She turned to Angie. "Uri not make sense. I understand not. He said about Chechnya."

Sergei looked at Finn. "Are you thinking what I'm thinking?"

"It's possible."

"What?" Angie demanded.

"During the Chechen War, there were rumors of war crimes. If Uri had some kind of proof against this general..." Sergei's voice trailed off.

"Is that even possible?" Angie asked.

"Stranger things have happened," Finn said.

"Where is Uri now?" Angie asked the question gently, sure she already knew the answer.

"He dead. He die on train tracks."

"Fuckers," Finn finally spoke up.

"How did you get away?"

"Uri hide me with prostitute. She give me card. I call man. He say I can be nanny."

"Dasha, what happened when you came to the United States?" Finn asked.

"Man and lady took my passport and said I be nanny. But then they took me to a place with many other girls. We not know what happening."

"So after you are with all the other girls, what happened?"

"They find out I pregnant and get very angry. I am scared they will beat me. But the lady said that it good thing. That is when they send me to the island."

"How long were you on the island?" Finn asked.

"Two. Maybe three months."

"Was it Rylie who sent her to the island?" Angie asked Finn.

"No. Rylie didn't know about the island," Finn told her. "Dasha, do you know where you were before they sent you to the island?"

"It was hot, like jungle."

"Mexico," Finn bit out. "She was part of the Guzman organization. They must have known about the Liu's baby selling business. God, the whole mess makes me want to kill them all over again."

Angie put her hand on his arm. He put his other hand on top of hers and took a deep breath.

"So she was in Mexico, to begin with?" Sergei asked.

"Yep. She was part of a huge human trafficking operation that spanned North America," Finn explained. "I only ever heard of the baby selling going on in Canada though."

"When they rescue us, many men from governments talk to us. Rylie nice and find Uncle Sergei, but government man say I must to go to Ukrainian Embassy. That is when I beg uncle to run away."

"Why didn't you just tell him why?" Angie asked.

"In my apartment, she saw pictures of me in my army uniform. She didn't realize that it was the US Army."

"Shit."

"Exactly, son." Sergei agreed with Finn. "It was a clusterfuck."

"Sergei, do you really think the general would be able to find her and do something to her here in the United States?" Angie asked.

She watched the old man rub his temple. "Yeah, I do. Somehow we have to out him before he gets to her."

"At least we know what we're up against. Thanks for finally explaining things." Finn reached out and patted Dasha's hand. She gave him a tremulous smile.

"I need to get her home."

8

AFTER THEY HAD LEFT, FINN WENT INTO THE GUEST BEDROOM.
He looked at his phone for a long time. He really wanted to
call Lydia, she would have the information he'd need about
the progress of the missing babies, but he missed his team.
God knew he thought the world of Lydia, but she wasn't one
of his brothers. Clint was Midnight Delta's computer guru,
so that's whose number he dialed.

"Hey, Clint. It's me–" Before he could continue, Clint
interrupted with a loud whoop.

"It's about fucking time. Wait 'til I tell everybody you're
back. God, we've been so worried about you. Are you good?"
What a loaded question. Finn sidestepped it.

"You probably know I'm in Austin," he said slowly.

"Nope," Clint said with a smile in his voice. "I didn't
track you. Lydia was pissed as hell when I told her we
weren't going to track you down. We had a hell of a fight."
There was a pause. "I want to thank you for that."

Finn was lost. "Why do you want to thank me?"

"For some of the best make up sex ever."

"You've been spending too much time with Drake." Finn shook his head, beginning to feel better that he'd called.

"Hell no. I've always been a fan of spending time with my woman. Anyway, I'm just trying to ease you back into the fold with sex talk, instead of immediately giving you the third degree. How am I doing?"

"You were doing good, but now you blew it."

"Well now that we're done with the kid gloves, how are you doing? Are you coming back?"

Finn thought about earlier in the week when he had lost it in the park. Then he remembered he had actually smiled with Angie. "There are bad days and good days."

"Thank fuck."

That floored him. "What are you talking about?"

"When you left, there were only bad days."

"Clint, I'm talking about a major freak-out."

"And that surprises you? Does it really, Finn? You've been walking a razor's edge for months. A major freak-out has been brewing. We've been expecting more than one. I have a question. Did you get yourself under control?"

"Yes," Finn reluctantly admitted.

"What was the good day?" Clint asked.

"It was nothing compared to the bad day."

"Just tell me," Clint coaxed. It rankled that he appreciated the care in Clint's tone, but he did. "Finn, answer me, buddy."

"There's this girl, well woman really, she actually gave me something to smile about."

"That's fucking awesome! Jesus, Finn, you smiled? For real?"

"Come on, it's not that big of a deal," Finn complained.

"Yeah, it really is." Clint sighed. "But you're not coming home, are you?"

"No, not yet."

"Okay. I am deducing you didn't call me because I'm the prettiest member of the team. You must need some information."

"You got it in one."

"What can I help you with?"

"I'm here in Austin with one of the mothers."

"You mean Dasha Koval. How did you know she was missing? Even with Melvin's help, we haven't found her. Rylie has been frantic." Finn didn't immediately answer the question, surprised Clint had to ask. His team had all met Declan, and Clint more than any of the others had an idea of the Shadow Alliance, and what it was about. He knew it had access to some freaky scary information.

"Think about it."

"I'm thinking." Then Clint whistled. "I've got it. This stinks to high heaven of Declan. I should have thought to ask you, but it just never occurred to me. I'm off my game. I'm a dumb shit, and you're good."

"Let's not get too crazy. Crazy being the key word in that sentence." He heard his friend stifle a laugh.

"Okay, you found Dasha. I can't wait to tell the team. What do you need our help with?"

"I need to know what progress you've made on finding the five missing babies, but most specifically, her baby."

"Hold on, I need to pull up some of the information." Finn listened to the normal sounds of Clint tapping on the computer keyboard. How often had he heard that sound? Too many times to number.

"Okay, there were two more reunited with their moms. As for Dasha's baby... We have a lead. We think her daughter is in Indianapolis."

"That's fantastic news. You know the name of the couple who bought her?"

"No. Just the city. But we think we'll have it narrowed down next week."

"Man, that's wonderful." Finn thought about Dasha and was overjoyed. The girl had been through hell. She needed to be reunited with her daughter.

"What about the final two babies?"

"We're still working every angle. We had to go on a mission, so it was just the women and Melvin working on it for a while. Lydia said that having me here actually helps. I was stunned she admitted it."

Finn's gut clenched. "You were on a mission? Where?"

"The Middle East."

"Was it bad?"

"When do they ever send us on a good mission, Finn?" Clint asked quietly.

And that was the crux of the matter.

"Is everyone safe?" Finn asked.

"If there had been something wrong with any of us, I would have gotten ahold of you within an hour."

"Thank you for that."

"You're one of us."

"No. I'm not. Not right now. I can't be."

"Don't say that."

"Trust me, it's not easy. I'm trying, man."

"If this was just a matter of grit and determination like BUD/S, you'd be here in San Diego. You'd be fine, and you would have been by my side in the middle of some God forsaken desert."

"Tell me about it," Finn said ruefully. "It feels like I'm fighting shadows that pop up out of thin air."

"If there is anything, and I mean anything, we can do, name it. We'll drop everything and be there."

"Fuck, I know that. But that was part of the problem. I needed to be on my own two feet without feeling like I was surrounded by people with their hands out ready to catch me. You know?"

"I could see that." He could almost hear his friend switch gears. "Tell me about the woman." Finn knew he wasn't asking about Dasha.

"Nope, you'll just be checking her out. I'm keeping her close to my vest right now."

"Hey, *I* wouldn't be checking her out."

"You, Lydia, Rylie. Does it really matter who? You'd have her third grade school picture by tomorrow." Clint let out a loud laugh.

"You sound so much better. But because you went dark, I'm giving Drake this number."

"You're an asshole," Finn said without heat.

"Yep."

Finn hung up and smiled.

ANGIE WAS ELATED when he told her the news. He asked her to call Dasha.

"Why me?"

"I've had enough emotional phone calls for one night."

"Honey, could you sit down beside me?" It was the first time she ever used an endearment. He liked hearing it. She lifted her legs just a little bit, and he sat down on the couch next to her and lifted her legs further so her knees could rest on top of his lap.

"It must have been really tough talking to one of your teammates. Which one was it? Mason?"

He gave her a surprised look. He guessed he shouldn't be surprised she had paid attention to his stories about his friends.

"No, it was Clint."

"Oh, the computer geek." She grinned. "He's the one who is married to Lydia, right?"

"They're just engaged." He took one of her feet and started to rub it. "But he's going to drag her down the aisle as soon as she finishes her master's. Actually, I'm surprised he's allowed her to wait."

"So how was it talking to Clint?" She sighed as he used his knuckles against the arch of her foot.

"They really understand what's going on with me. They were fine letting me have the space I needed."

"Really?" she prodded.

She was perceptive, this woman who was tired up and wounded, curled up on the couch.

"I wouldn't be fine letting someone who is close to me just take off. If they were hurting, that's when I would want them closest to me."

Finn sighed. "There was some of that. But they also respected my need to work things out on my own."

"You have some great friends."

"They're my brothers. They were just on a mission. I know if I had been home and tried to go with them, I would have been a liability."

"Other foot." He looked at her. She lifted her left foot and pointed at it. "Rub my other foot."

"Yes, ma'am." He suspected she was using a stalling tactic.

"I thought you did pretty good at the park. I know you'll

think I'm just saying that because I want to kiss you again, and maybe do other things besides kissing. But I really do think you handled yourself really well." He stopped rubbing her foot.

"What planet do you come from?"

"Here me out, okay? Yeah, sure, I saw you freak out, but I also saw you pull yourself together pretty damn quickly. I've been reading up on this. Dasha triggered you, but you were able to deal with her within minutes after your episode, that is significant."

He didn't say anything, so she prodded him with her toe, and he started rubbing again.

"Maybe you have a point," Finn finally admitted.

"I do."

"But not having an episode is key. I can't do my job if I'm not under complete control."

"This was a unique set of circumstances. How often are you confronted by crying Ukrainian teenage girls?" Angie teased him.

"About once a month," he said with a straight face.

She reached out to hit him and then gasped with pain.

"Dammit, Angie, you need to be careful. Is it time for another pain pill?"

"Maybe," she admitted.

He got up from the couch and brought her back a glass of water and a tablet.

"Thank you."

"It's time to get you to bed. Put your hands around my neck." He said and picked her up and took her to the guest room.

"Did I ever tell you that I love how you carry me around?"

"That works out pretty well since I really love holding

you." He pulled back the coverlet, and placed her on the bed, then he went over to her suitcase. "What do you want to sleep in?" He watched as she blushed. It was cute, but then it bothered him.

"Angie, what can I do to make this easier? I know we were intimate earlier but are you going to resent needing my help to undress now?" She pressed her hands to her cheeks.

"It's stupid."

He sat on the side of the bed. "No, it's not. Feelings are never stupid, they're just feelings." She gave him a shy smile.

"Thank you."

"You're welcome. Now how can I make this better?"

"You just did. Get my Longhorn sleepshirt, and help me in to it, okay?"

"Your wish is my command." He made brisk work of getting her out of her tunic and into her sleep shirt. But as he was smoothing it down over her back, right above her bottom, he saw it. His hands stilled.

"Finn?"

"How did this happen?" he asked in a careful voice.

Keep it together, Crandall.

"It was a long time ago. I was young and stupid."

"How?"

Angie let out a sigh. "Help me under the covers." Like she might shatter, he settled her onto the mattress and pulled up the covers. She shimmied out of her pants and handed them to him.

"Tell me."

"It was only twelve stitches." She smiled.

He continued to hold her gaze, unamused.

"It wasn't because I was on the job, so we can't blame that."

"I'm listening."

She pulled at the cover, and he plucked her hand up in his. "Just tell me," he said.

"I was getting gas. One stall over a kid jumps this older lady who was pumping gas. He had a knife. I apprehended him."

Finn's hand tightened. "That's a bad place for a knife wound."

Angie looked down as he laced their fingers together. "I was lucky. It didn't hit anything vital. No surgery."

"Dammit woman, what am I going to do with you?"

She pulled his hand to her lips. "Let me play in the big leagues?" she asked hopefully.

He did a double take, then he shook his head. "You are something else, Ms. Donatelli. Can I get you anything?"

"I'm good." She smiled at him.

"Okay. I'm going to leave both of our bedroom doors open tonight. I'll be able to hear you if you need anything."

"Thanks, Finn."

ON THE THIRD DAY, Finn gave in and agreed to take Angie into the office.

"You know I'm fine," she cajoled.

"That's a load of crap."

"You know I'm getting on your nerves."

"Well there is that," he relented. Angie laughed. She really enjoyed the man, but being in such close quarters with him, and not jumping his bones, was getting more and more difficult.

"What?"

"What do you mean, *what*?"

"You were looking at me funny," he said.

"Just take me to the office. I dressed myself and everything." It had been a major pain in the ass, but she had managed to do it. Hell, she'd gone all out, even applied makeup and lip gloss.

He opened his mouth to lodge what she knew was going to be another protest when she stopped him.

"You know it requires a security check to get into the office building. They have a picture of Paul Jackson, and they won't let him up. I'm not leaving the office until you pick me up at two o'clock. I'm only going to be at the office for five hours." He shut his mouth.

When they got to the apartment parking lot, he ushered her to his car.

"I really think you should only stay there four hours."

"We agreed on five. I promise if I get tired after three hours, I'll call you." He gave her a glance as he started the car.

"Seriously, I will. I'm not going to jeopardize my recovery. I have meetings today and tomorrow with Anders Microtech. I really need to be there."

"I know. You've explained it to me—multiple times."

By the time they got to her office building, she was breathing heavily, but not from pain. It was the parking garage. She hadn't considered it. Finn drove in and hit the button for the ticket and waited for the gate to lift up. She could barely take in air. He caught on immediately.

"Angie. We're leaving. It's not a problem. We're getting out of here now."

She heard him swearing under his breath, calling himself every kind of idiot, as he sped around the garage and exited in record time.

As soon as they were back on the street, she could breathe again. He found a spot to parallel park, and came over to the passenger side and opened the door.

"Do you want to go back home?" he asked. Her eyes were closed. She didn't want him to see her tears. God, this must be how he felt twenty-four seven. It sucked donkey-balls. She opened her eyes and tried to smile.

"Yes, I want to go back home. No, I'm not. I'm going to the office. Thanks for getting me out of the garage so quickly. It scared the hell out of me."

"I wasn't thinking. Being the king of flashbacks, I should have thought of it. I'm a dumb shit."

"Don't pick on my guy." He brushed a kiss on her cheek. She quickly turned her head, capturing his mouth. Heat flared. The last of the fear dissipated.

"Let's get you inside. Remember I'll be back at one o'clock." She laughed.

"Okay, one o'clock, you pushy man."

BEFORE HE WENT BACK to the searches on Ukrainian generals, Finn decided to go on a desperately needed run. He hadn't been on one since Angie had started staying with him. His habit of early morning runs had gotten him through a lot. Besides the burn, it helped him to zone out, and eventually, it focused his thinking. The last three mornings, he had felt cloudy. And needy. And achy. And horny.

He desperately needed to run. So he upped his normal fifteen mile run to twenty miles.

Angie. Clint. Dasha. He still remembered Lou Donatelli's calming voice after the episode in the park. He'd googled the man. He had been promoted to a lieutenant in the Marines while serving in Vietnam. Having him say there was no shame in freaking out had helped.

Still, it had taken until mile seventeen before he managed to clean out all of the shit and focus on what was important—Angie's health. Then he went through another mile kicking his ass for taking her through the parking garage. The last two miles he replayed the kiss and the promise in her eyes.

Yep, Ms. Donatelli was definitely healing. She had worn strawberry lip gloss. Maybe it was time to make dinner for her. He was mulling over potential menus as he reached the parking lot of the apartment complex. Declan was leaning against his El Camino. At least, there was a pink bakery box at his feet.

"You didn't just let yourself in?" Finn commented as he jogged up to him.

"It seemed rude," Declan said.

"That's never stopped you in the past."

"Angie might have left her underthings drying in the kitchen. I didn't want my sensibilities upset." Declan bent down and picked up the box and held it out to Finn. "I came bearing gifts."

"Maple bars?"

"I'd be a pretty crap friend if they weren't."

"Okay, you can come in." Finn headed towards his apartment, certain Declan would follow him. When he let himself in, he headed towards the kitchen and plugged in the coffee maker.

"For God's sake, let me make the coffee. Go shower. You stink."

He eyed Declan. "Gotten kind of picky, haven't you?" he asked his childhood friend.

The man raised an eyebrow and pushed him out of the way of the coffee maker. It was nice some things didn't change. Even after saying shitty things to him, and pulling a knife on him, they were solid.

He spent a couple of extra minutes in the shower because it smelled like strawberries thanks to Angie's bath products. God, he had it bad. But he drew the line at actually using her shampoo. By the time he was dressed and in the kitchen, he smelled the divine scent of coffee. The pastries were set out on plates beside the coffee mugs on the table.

"What, no doilies?"

"You're a fucking sailor. You're lucky I gave you a plate."

Finn rolled his eyes. "S.E.A.L. It stands for Sea, Air and Land, you pasty faced MIC asshole."

"That'd be Military Intelligence Corp. Intelligence. You should be appreciative of this, considering I come bearing gifts." Declan grinned.

"You got my message. You have something on the general?" Finn grinned.

"Wait just a damned minute. Did I just see the surly sailor smile?"

"SEAL."

"I'll call you whatever you want me to, as long as I see you smile again. Does this have something to do with the pretty Angie Donatelli? If yes, I *so* have to meet her."

"Let's just stick to business." Finn picked up his doughnut and took a bite.

"It is because of Angie."

"Cut the shit, McAllister. I want to focus on your findings. We have a shit storm brewing."

Declan sat across from Finn and picked up his mug of coffee. "I'll say you do. Vlad Lutsenko is as bad as it gets."

Finn snorted. He'd seen the bad, badder, and baddest.

"I know, I know. Bad comes in so many crappy flavors these days. But this guy has been under investigation for war crimes. He is bad news. He has been turning Odessa upside down looking for Dasha Koval. He knows she's in the states, and all Embassy business has been focused on one goal—to find her."

"She doesn't deserve this."

"Who does?"

Finn pictured Dasha in the park. Her eyes filled with tears as she described those hours she'd had with her daughter. He thought of her in his apartment explaining about Uri, and how she had escaped the Ukraine just to fall into the arms of the predators here in America.

He took another sip of coffee, and it hit him wrong. A ball of fire punched through his gut. He needed some milk to soothe away the heat. He lurched up and slammed open the refrigerator to get the carton. He pushed through the contents, intent on the milk when his arm hit the bottle of hot sauce, and it knocked over.

Everything stopped. Not one second elapsed. Not one mote of dust floated by. Not one breath of air escaped his lungs.

A small curious part of his brain was operating. Where had that bottle come from? Oh yeah, someone had stocked the fridge before he arrived, and he'd never seen it before. Oh look, it's rolling. But that observer voice was very faint, and far away.

The bottle of hot sauce rolled off the shelf and crashed to the floor, his ears heard the plastic bounce, but his eyes saw glass shatter and red liquid cover the floor. It looked like blood. He couldn't look away from the imaginary spread of blood as it pooled on the kitchen floor.

Finn gulped hard, trying not to throw up. The taste of cayenne peppers filled his mouth. Was a girl whimpering for mercy?

Dammit! No! He was in his kitchen.

"Finn? Can you hear me?"

He jumped at the hand on his shoulder. He heard the whimper again and realized it was him.

"Give me a minute." He closed his eyes tight and then opened them again. He looked down and saw the plastic bottle of hot sauce laying on its side on the kitchen floor. But damn, the carton of milk had fallen over and spilled.

"Sit down, buddy." Declan's emerald eyes were bright with compassion. "Come on, just sit down for a second." Declan maneuvered Finn into the kitchen chair where he'd been sitting.

Finn pushed the heel of his hand into his right eye.

"You did well. You kept it together." Declan's voice was soothing. What the fuck was up with that?

"I don't need to be played. Don't talk to me like I'm a child."

"I'm not. I'm talking to you like you're my friend. I'm talking to you like you talked to me four years ago. Remember?"

Well, that put him in his place, now didn't it?

Declan stepped over the mess on the floor and snagged another container of milk from the fridge and poured Finn a glass.

"Drink your milk, and tell me how you managed to process your way out of that so fast." Finn took the glass.

"What? No cookies?" Finn was thankful he managed to sound like a sarcastic asshole.

"I brought you fucking maple bars." The man had a point. Finn turned and got another doughnut out of the box, took a big bite, and drank half of the glass of milk. Finally, the taste of cayenne pepper was washed away, and his stomach didn't feel like a dragon trying to claw its way out of his guts. Now, if he could just fix it so the last five minutes could be erased, he'd be good.

He threw down the rest of the doughnut and covered his twitching eye. Dammit, he needed to get his shit together. He really wanted Dec to think he had processed and was okay, instead of feeling like he was ready to fly apart again. When were things going to stop setting him off?

He watched Declan's slow movements as he sopped up every drop of milk off the floor with paper towels. It seemed to be taking him for-fucking-ever. Then Finn finally realized Dec was giving him time to get himself together. Which just made his eye twitch even faster.

"Get up off the floor. I'm fine."

"The last thing you need is the smell of sour milk mutating from underneath the kitchen counters." Declan went over to the sink and wet some towels, and then swiped them around the perimeter of the floor. He then threw them away and washed his hands before coming back to the table.

"Any doughnuts left?" Declan asked.

"One," Finn answered. "But you can't have it. Crazy boy gets the last doughnut."

"Doesn't work in this case," Declan said as he opened the box and grabbed the maple bar and took a bite. "You're only fucked in the head and not really crazy, so the rule doesn't apply."

Finn's gut unclenched. Granted he still wasn't feeling all that great, but the knots he'd been tied up in for the last few months, loosened. But then his thoughts began to swirl angrily.

Dec thought he was fucked in the head, did he? Well, he knew up close and personal, just what a batshit fucked-up son-of-a-bitch Declan McAllister was. How dare Dec try to pass judgement on him? How dare he?

"Finn stay with me."

Declan was gripping his shoulders. Finn saw the fierce gleam of determination in his friend's eyes.

"I'm right here. I'm fine," Finn said through gritted teeth.

"Don't say another word. One more lie comes out of your mouth, then I'll be forced to knock you on your ass."

"Give it your best shot Army."

"I told you, I came here on a mission of mercy, seems like bad form to hit a man while he's down."

A half cough, half laugh wheezed out of Finn's mouth.

"Excuse me? Did I just hear you laugh?"

"Even on your best day, and my worst, you couldn't take me. Not even as a kid." Back then it had been close, *damn close*, but Finn had always won. Then Finn had gone through BUD/S, and Declan had been toast ever since.

"I think today is finally that day, Swabbie. Now tell me what the fuck is really going on. Tell me why you haven't gone to see a shrink, you're smarter than this. You went to one when your Granddad was diagnosed with Alzheimer's."

"That was different. I did it to convince Mom it was okay to go." Finn squeezed his eyes shut. "The base counselor was kind and good at her job, but I'm sure as hell not telling her my sins."

"Interesting word."

"Fuck you, McAllister."

Finn got up and pulled the dishes off the table and slammed them in the sink. "You weren't there. Nobody but me, those fucking 'dead men walking' and the girls that I couldn't protect."

"Seems to me they're alive today," Declan pointed out quietly.

Finn gripped the corner of the counter. He wasn't having a flashback, it was a clear-as-a-bell memory. He saw Penelope in the corner of the farmhouse kitchen puking her guts up with the other girls huddled around her. Howard and Mike standing there laughing. He wiped the sweat from his brow. His breathing was shallow, but then he took three deep breaths and got himself back under control. Control being his watchword.

"They might be alive, but they're scarred."

"Have you even bothered to look at their files?"

"I don't need to. I was there."

"I'm talking about now. Have you looked into their records since they've gone home or assimilated to the US?"

Finn turned around to look at his friend who was standing in the middle of the kitchen. Dec's hair was in disarray from where he had been raking his fingers through it, a sure sign he was upset.

"What do you know about the girls?"

"Apparently, more than you do. Hell Finn, the girl you're so worried about, is in San Antonio."

"Who?"

"Penelope." Yep, Declan knew. Finn hadn't been sure which girl Declan was talking about. Even though nowhere on any of the records was there any mention of Liliya, the girl who had offered to go down on him so that she could escape. The only mention in the reports had been of Penelope, who he'd held down so others could force hot sauce down her throat. Still, this was Declan McAllister. He probably knew the last time the Russian president took a dump.

"Finn, who did you think I meant?"

"I worry about all of the girls from the farmhouse," Finn covered. Declan gave him a considering glance.

"Penelope is with Grace Preston in San Antonio. She took in three of the displaced girls." If he'd bothered to pay attention for the last month, he would have known that. Now he had to admit that he had been keeping all of this information at arms-length.

"Who else?"

"I can't believe how far deeply your head has been buried in the sand." Declan rolled his shoulders and walked over to the table and sat down. "Please give me credit for saying sand and not ass." Finn glared at Declan, who just shrugged.

"Are they doing okay?" Finn wished he could have sounded less concerned.

"For God's sake, Finn, if you were that worried, you should have asked Clint the other night on the phone." He went and sat back down at the table next to Declan.

"Clint and I were discussing other things, so tell me about the girls from the farmhouse."

"Rylie and Lydia have been working on matching up the missing babies and their mothers, while Sophia and Beth have coordinated finding places for the girls who can't go back to their original homes."

"So Beth arranged for three girls to go to San Antonio, to Jack's parent's ranch?" Finn asked.

"Exactly. Those girls from the farmhouse are doing well. I promise you. I don't know their names. You know that Sophia and Beth are doing what they can for them. Those women are a force to be reckoned with."

"Yeah they are," he agreed. They looked across the table at one another. "So just how much do you know about Midnight Delta?" Finn asked.

"I basically gave the unit a colonoscopy."

The corner of his mouth kicked up. "So you unearthed all of our shit."

"Thank God, your sense of humor is coming back, I thought we would need to do a medical transplant or some such shit. But you still need help," Declan said the last words gently.

"I know. I just need a little more space. You of all people should understand that. I gave it to you when you needed it."

"Only because you couldn't find me," Declan said as he kicked back his chair.

Finn raised his eyebrow. "Believe what you need to believe, McAllister."

"Okay, I'll back off...for now. Aren't you supposed to call you mother today?"

Goddamit, was there some kind of GPS listening device stuck up his ass, Finn wondered.

"I'm supposed to call her tomorrow. But, yeah, I'm going to call her today. I miss her and Rebecca. Now that you've eaten all of my maple bars get the hell out of my apartment."

"I'll be back," Declan said as he got up and headed for the door.

"Never doubted it," Finn muttered. He picked up his phone and dialed his mom's number as he watched the door close behind Declan.

DECLAN DROVE TOWARDS THE AIRPORT. He figured he would book a flight when he got there. He hadn't been sure how long this visit with Finn would take. He'd packed a bag in case he needed to spend a couple of nights, even if he would have been stuck on the couch. As far as Declan was concerned, Finn was family, and you did whatever was necessary to take care of your family when they were in trouble.

Finn had always been stoic in the past. He endured a lot and had been a rock. Declan remembered when Ginger had lost the baby. Finn had convinced himself it was his fault she'd gotten drunk for the umpteenth time, slipped, fell, and miscarried. Even though he had done everything possible to support her and get her the help, she needed to stop drinking. To this day he still thought *he* was to blame for *her* actions. Taking the blame for things was Finn's M.O. It was obvious he was feeling just as guilty for the horror at the farmhouse, when in actuality he had saved that girl. But of course, his friend would never see it that way.

Declan knew what was going on with Finn. It was like seeing a mirror image of himself from four years ago. Finn had tamped down his emotions so deep that they were bubbling up like magma from a volcano. Throw in all of the missions he'd been on over the years and the recent combat injury of his lieutenant and 'bam', there he was.

That flashback Finn had at the apartment had been intense. It had him breaking out into a sweat, remembering some of his own. Declan winced thinking about the last assignment he worked for Military Intelligence. It hadn't just blurred the lines between right and wrong, it had smashed them to bits. It had sent him reeling into a black hole that he might never have come out of if he hadn't gotten a whole hell of a lot of love and support. That's why he intended to be there for the man he considered his brother.

He would continue to have eyes and ears on Finn. He'd

be back. In the meantime, he was really worried and really happy about the stuff going on between Dasha and the general. Worried because Vlad was a scary bastard, and Declan guessed this could get really ugly, really quickly. He was happy because, at his core, Finn was a protector and a warrior. Having a mission to focus on was perfect to help heal Finn's heart—at least temporarily. Declan still intended to get him into therapy and at least one 'share circle' with sex being optional.

Declan's phone vibrated for the forty-seventh time. He knew Brannon had things under control so he could ignore it. He'd check his messages when he got to the airport. He was itching to get back to Paraguay. He and his team were on the cusp of making real headway, and considering how utterly wretched the conditions were, he was thrilled.

Before his visit with Finn, Declan had been debating whether to call Mason Gault. Then he realized he didn't have to because Finn had reached out to Clint Archer. He wondered if Midnight Delta had gone soft or stupid when they let Finn leave until he had heard the conversation between Finn and Clint. It was obvious the SEALs had respected Finn's request for distance and had given him the space he desired. They probably would say it was unethical that he had listened to Finn's conversation. Well, he hadn't gone soft or stupid, he would push a whole slew of boundaries to make sure the people he loved were safe.

He had liked it when Clint said that they could have gotten ahold of Finn within an hour if they really needed him. That satisfied Declan. Because he had a plan. He always had plans. There was the hourly plan, the daily plan, the weekly, the monthly, the yearly, the current mission plan, and then there was the long term plan.

The long term plan was for all of Midnight Delta, and

their women, to one day belong to him. The Shadow Alliance needed these men and women. In the meantime, he'd keep an eye on his friend from afar. If there were any signs Finn's state was getting worse, he'd be back in an instant.

9

Angie had been exhausted by the time he got her to the apartment.

"I can't wait to tell you about the meeting." She yawned again.

"It sounds like it went great."

"I can't believe I fell asleep in the car," she said for the third time as he helped her sit on the couch. "I don't need your help anymore."

"Humor me." She slumped against the pillows. He could see gooseflesh on her arms, and grabbed the afghan off the back of the couch to place over her.

"Seriously. I'm not." She yawned again. "Okay, maybe a short nap." She laughed.

"That gives me time to get the vegetables prepped for dinner." She was already stretching out against the pillows with her eyes closed. She looked gorgeous.

He went back to his computer and called up the information on Big Bad Vlad. He was currently in the United States getting ready to give a speech and attend some meetings. It seemed like a weird coincidence to Finn.

The ever detailed Declan had also provided information on the baby daddy. He looked so young, while Vlad looked like someone's worst nightmare come to life. He was in charge of the Russian Special Forces group for most of his career. While he had been part of the Russian Army, it had been rumored he had decimated a Chechen village, and some of his officers had reported him. Those officers were never seen or heard from again. Vlad had a long scar over his left eye, it was said to have been the result of an assassination attempt by one of his most trusted men.

Now that he had the information on the general, it was far past time to face the music of his actions. His fingers actually trembled as he typed the message to Lydia asking for updates on the girls from the farmhouse.

Instantly there was a reply.

What do you want? Who do you want information on? Penelope?

His fingers froze above the keyboard. He didn't want to mention Liliya as well.

All of them.

Beth and Sophia have been sending me updates. They are doing great. Well, except for one.

Finn shut his eyes, imagining the worst.

What's going on?

I'll just forward you their e-mails. You can read it all.

He thanked her and waited. Less than a minute went by, and he had all of the information he needed on the girls. Sophia was ridiculously thorough, she kept a daily diary. Beth had chatty letters going on between her and Grace Preston.

Penelope and two other girls were staying at the ranch in San Antonio. Grace had arranged for a tutor to come over daily to teach them English, as well as a psychologist. The three girls were flourishing.

Finn was astounded to read that Penelope was taking a leadership role over the girls, coaxing them to ride horses and work in the garden. Then like a bolt of lightning in a clear blue sky it occurred to Finn that of course, she would be the leader. She was the one who had tried to escape from the farmhouse. What's more, she had tried to escape again when they were at the mansion for the auction. Drake had told him that this girl was a fighter, and he had never realized it until now. He had only seen her as a victim. She would hate for him to picture her that way. He was an idiot.

He eagerly read through the other e-mails, wanting to see how Liliya was doing. Praying she was not the one having a hard time. He soon saw that Liliya had been sent back to her home in Russia where she was living with her older brother and sister-in-law. Thank God.

He vaguely remembered the pretty, shy brunette who was not doing well. She wasn't speaking. Sophia had her staying with some friends of hers in San Clemente. Finn knew the older couple that had taken her in and knew that they would offer a great deal of love and attention. Finn whispered a prayer that she would soon be doing better.

Then a text came in. He smiled grimly. This was a call he needed to take outside. He went over to the couch and made sure Angie was still doing okay. He tucked the blanket closer around her and stepped outside so he could call Lou.

"When will he be there?" Finn asked.

"What, no hello?" the old man complained.

"Hello Lou, how are you doing? It's been pretty hot lately, hasn't it? Now when will he be there?"

"I'm not sure this is a great idea."

Finn laughed. "That is the biggest load of bullshit I've ever heard, Marine. You're just upset you're not doing it."

"He goes to the strip club on payday, which will be this Friday. He and his friends usually get kicked out because they get so out of control. The bartender calls them a cab."

"This should work. I'd take you with me, but he'd be able to ID you in a line-up. He doesn't know me."

"Thanks for doing this Finn, I owe you one."

"Lou," Finn said warningly.

"Oh, it's like that. Got to say, I was kind of hoping."

"We'll see if your granddaughter feels that way. But I'm planning on convincing her."

"I didn't raise a stupid girl."

"No, you certainly didn't. Stubborn, but not stupid. I need to get back inside."

"I'll text you the time and place."

"Thanks, Lou. You'll need to come up with a diversion for Angie on Friday night."

"I've got it handled."

"Thanks."

"No, thank you, son." Finn hung up and went back to the apartment.

He opened the door and went directly to the couch. Angie was muttering in her sleep. She looked beautiful, and she was smiling. Maybe she was having happy dreams. He hoped so. She'd been killing him lately. But he was pretty sure the feeling was mutual based on all of the boulder-sized hints she'd been dropping. She wasn't any happier sleeping alone than he was.

Once again, he smoothed the afghan on her, then went into the kitchen to prep for dinner. He always found cooking soothing. And, he had gone to the dumpster and thrown out the damn bottle of hot sauce. Maybe that made him a pussy, but he needed more bombshells in his life like he needed a hole in the head.

———————

ANGIE STRETCHED, and for the first time in days, it hardly hurt at all. Okay, it still hurt like a bitch, but she wasn't going to admit it. She had plans. Admitting she was hurting was not going to get her what she wanted. She threw off the blanket and meandered into the kitchen.

"That smells really good, what is it?"

"Chicken stir-fry and noodles."

Her mouth watered. She slid by him, a lot closer than necessary, to grab a water glass out of the cupboard.

"Let me get that." He handed her the glass, and lightly touched her waist in the process.

She put her hand on top of his. "You can press harder. I'm not made of glass." She grinned.

Finn frowned. "Are you trying to tell me you're not in pain still? Because I'm not buying it. I've had broken ribs."

"Just one rib is broken. One," she reminded him. "And my waist is fine."

"I saw your hip."

Angie pressed her finger to his lips. "I just wanted some water." He raised an eyebrow. "Okay, and to brush up against you. I *am* doing better, except my neediness level is off the chart."

He gently cupped her hips and brought her closer. She felt his heat, his strength, his desire. She wiggled against his erection. He hissed in a breath. "My neediness level is pretty damn high too. I think it needs to be measured."

Angie blinked, and threw back her head and laughed. He moved, thrust his fingers into her hair, and drew her in for a kiss, the likes of which she had never experienced. His lips were a hard, hungry wonder making her open and beg for more.

His tongue thrust in, and her head spun with carnal bliss. She sucked him deeper, scraping him with her teeth, enjoying the growl that sent ripples to her core. He plunged in again, and she nipped his tongue. His large hand gripped her ass causing her nipples to harden and her pussy to weep. She jerked away, her eyes wide.

"Bedroom." Was that husky purr her voice?

Her Boy Scout kissed the top of her head and turned to make sure all the burners were off. Then she was in his arms, and he was striding to her room.

"It smells like a strawberry field in here, but I know one thing that will smell even better." She froze. Oh, he was not going to be like any of the polite Southern boy lovers of her past.

He set her down beside the bed. She crossed her arms in front so she could take off her blouse.

"Oh no, I get to unwrap my present."

"Faster this way." Then she did a stupid thing and tried to hurry, wincing in pain as she pulled off her top.

"Dammit, Angie," came the muffled roar. "We do this my way, or not at all. Are we clear?"

"Yes, sir." Would he stop if she saluted? No, he wouldn't, not with the way he stared at her cleavage. Thank God for the power of boobs.

"You're beautiful."

"You've seen me before. As a matter of fact, I wasn't wearing a bra."

He looked up at her and shook his head. "That can be easily rectified." Finn unclasped her bra and peeled it down her arms. Then he knelt in front of her, and cupped both breasts, and licked a nipple. Her legs lost all strength, and she would have fallen except for his fast action. He had her lying on the bed and stripped out of her slacks and panties in under a minute.

"Beautiful," he reiterated.

Angie was still trembling from the one caress. He pulled his shirt off with that manly over the back, one armed tug, and she finally got to see the most gorgeous chest she had ever seen in her life. She held out her arms.

ANGIE STILL HAD BRUISING on her hip, and her ribcage was still wrapped with tape. In no way, shape or form did it detract from her beauty. But it did make him very conscious of the fact that the formidable Angie Donatelli needed to be treated like spun glass.

"Now, Finn," she commanded. That stopped him. What? She expected him to climb on board? What kind of lovers had she had in the past? He cupped her ankle and then trailed the backs of his fingers up the inside of her leg. Higher and higher, closer and closer to the bare mound that beckoned like a candle at midnight.

She squirmed, and parted her legs further so he was tempted, and finally, he was there. Just a touch and she gasped his name. Delicate flesh he had to taste and savor. He needed this closeness like he needed his next breath. Finn nuzzled, and licked, as she shuddered and sighed. Carefully, he coaxed her over the edge, exalting in her cry of pleasure.

"Now, Finn," she pleaded. He stepped off the bed, shucked off his jeans, and grabbed a condom. He laid down beside her and gathered her close. She was trembling, and so was he. For the first time in months, he was close to finding something he needed, something clean and pure. She turned in his arms.

All pleading was gone. Her fingers traced his cheekbones. She kissed his forehead. His eyelids, his lips. She was killing him. "You've given me so much, Finn. You don't see it. But I've never had someone stand beside me and want to protect me before."

"I don't understand," he whispered. Her skin was so soft as he touched the shell of her ear.

"Of course, you don't. Because you're just being Finn Crandall. You're the man I'm coming to love." Finn froze, and she immediately felt it. "Damn, too much, too soon, wasn't it? How about the man I'm coming to lust?" She gave him a cheeky grin, and his heart lurched. Ginger had made love a four letter word, he needed to reclaim it.

"Love, Angie. I like the word love a whole lot better. Lust is good, but love is what's happening in this room—in this bed."

"Then why did you tense up?"

"Bad memories. But you're chasing them away."

"I'm glad. Do you want to talk about it?" Her brown eyes a soft liquid brown.

He needed another kind of intimacy right then. "Later, I want this kind of love, first." He bent down and parted her lips with his. The flavor of strawberries exploded across his senses. She stroked him with one hand, while the other pulled the condom wrapper from his hand.

"I can't wait, I need you." Her thumb glided over his tip, and he was close to losing it.

"Slow, I need this to last. We only have one first time, lady, I want to savor it."

Her breath hitched, and she kissed his chin. He brushed

the arch of her brow and gazed into her eyes. Then he stroked downward until he was once again cupping her breast, rolling her nipple to a swollen point.

"So good," she sighed softly, was there pain in her sigh? He bent, and took the crest in his mouth, holding her gently down on the bed, and forcing her to keep still for his ministrations.

"Let me move."

"No. It hurts you."

"Staying still hurts more."

She had so much to learn. He squeezed, and she cried out. "Just lie there and enjoy this. I need to touch you, please you. I can't stand the thought of you in pain." He tenderly clasped her delicate flesh, loving how her breath caught.

"Again."

He obliged, and then his thumb rasped over her nipple, again and again. She made a small move, and he stopped.

"Finn?"

"You move, and I stop, that's the game."

"I don't like that game." He softly grasped her nipple with his teeth, and she shrilled with pleasure as his tongue worked the nub. The moment she moved he stopped.

"I. Hate. This. Game."

"I don't want you to be in pain."

"There's a part of me that is painfully achy. Painfully empty." She smiled. He licked her nipple one last time, and then kissed her beautiful smile. She drew him in, he gloried in the closeness and realized she was right. He found the wrapper, and she helped to get the protection in place, doubling the amount of time it took with four hands attempting the task.

Their laughter filled the bedroom, then they looked at one another and realized the moment had finally come.

"Finn?" her voice trembled.

"I have you." Had it ever been more important? He watched her languid expression of joy as he slowly slid home. She tried to lift, but he held her still. "Just squeeze baby." He felt her clutch, and sweat broke out all over his body. She gave him a dazed smile as she clenched in a sweet rhythm with his every thrust.

"This is incredible," she breathed.

"It's you. You take my breath away, lady." Faster, but still careful, he moved. She gripped him tighter and made the sweetest sounds of passion. Her nails dug into his ass, as she pushed upwards, and he thrust harder and faster, loving her tight pulsing.

He watched as her eyes glazed over and she started to tremble. He continued his loving strokes, and watched as she flew, then he followed. When he came back to himself, he realized he had finally found redemption.

"Finn, is that your phone?"

Finn felt like he was coming out of a drugged sleep. When was the last time he had slept so deeply? He couldn't remember. Angie was a warm blessing by his side, he was loathe to leave her. What time was it? His internal alarm said probably only nine in the evening.

"You must be starved."

"I could eat." She reached down his body, and he grabbed her hand. Their eyes met, and they laughed.

"Trying to get into trouble, Ms. Donatelli?"

"I could eat you with a spoon, Mr. Crandall." God, he needed to get out of bed and get her dinner.

"Your phone?"

"I'll get that. But first, do you need help getting dressed?"

"I'll manage. You get your phone and the food. I'll take care of my clothes."

Finn pulled on his jeans and checked out what they had that would be fast to cook, after throwing out the dinner. He nuked yesterday's burritos and whipped up a salad. He got her the sweet tea she liked since she was still taking pain pills, then he checked his phone. He recognized Drake's number and figured he'd call him back tomorrow.

He watched Angie carefully all through dinner until she finally put down her silverware and looked at him. "What, do I have food in my teeth?"

"Huh?"

"You're looking at me like I'm a bug under a microscope. I thought I might have food in my teeth."

He gave her a sheepish grin. "I just wanted to make sure you were moving okay. I didn't want you to be hurting."

"You know you could try this really weird thing called asking."

He flushed. "Yeah, I guess I could. Are you hurting?"

She laughed. "A little, but I was kind of hoping for a replay anyway. Can I tempt you?"

"Not if you're hurting."

She picked up her fork and starting quietly eating her food.

"Hey, I thought you said you were only hurting a little bit. What's wrong?"

"I think I shouldn't have opened my big mouth in bed." He scrambled to keep up. Dammit, from everything he knew about Angie, he should have known she would take his response as a rejection. *And he damn well better not say it was him, and not her. Time to man up, Crandall.*

"Her name was Ginger."

Angie set down her fork and pushed her plate away. "The woman who made love a four letter word for you."

"Yeah, she didn't really know the meaning of the word. She used it to try and control me." Angie didn't say anything, she just tilted her head for him to continue. Finn swallowed. "I got her pregnant," he said baldly.

"Did *you* love *her*?"

"Not at all. I'd only known her for a week. The condom broke."

"Damn, when was this?"

"It was while I was taking college courses. She wanted to get married, and I agreed. It was a stupid decision. We didn't even know each other, but I thought it was the right thing to do. We got engaged, but she was the world's biggest party girl."

"Like how, Finn?" He could see Angie guessed the truth.

"I don't think there were drugs involved, but she drank all of the time. I tried to get her help. I arranged an intervention with her family. Nothing worked." Finn remembered Ginger's rage. Angie got up and came around to his side of the table.

She twirled her finger. He moved his chair back, and she sat down on his lap and wrapped her arm around his neck. "I need to be close to you before you tell me the rest."

"I don't know if I can," he said hoarsely.

She sat there for a long time with her head resting on his chest.

"After the intervention, she told me she didn't want to see me ever again. I respected her wishes, to begin with, but I started calling after two weeks and leaving messages. Three weeks after the intervention she called me. I was at the base in Coronado. It's an hour from her apartment. It was raining. She said she needed a ride. I told her I'd be there and to wait for me," his voice was thick with emotion.

Angie cuddled closer. "Finish it."

"There was a wreck on the freeway. I was late. She was drunk again. She left the apartment and slipped down the stairs and...and..."

Angie squeezed him close. "She lost the baby, didn't she?"

"My son. My son died. I failed him. I failed both of them."

"Finn."

He shook so hard, if she hadn't been holding on so tight, she might have fallen off his lap. Dammit, he needed to get himself under control.

"Finn, look at me," she said as she cupped his cheek. He'd never seen such soft midnight brown eyes in his life. They shimmered with the tears he couldn't shed.

"Angie," he breathed. "I don't know what to do."

"Your son knows you love him." He'd never taken a harder punch in his life.

"How?"

"He's yours. He's a part of you. He knows. And you know something else?"

"What?" he was scared to ask.

"He loves you too."

The tears started to fall, and somehow Angie managed to keep him from flying apart.

10

—————

He looked at his phone again. Another call from Drake. He set it down. He just wasn't ready to talk to him yet. He watched Angie's sleeping form. She really was a miracle. Somehow telling her the story made him feel a little lighter.

He knew he had to take her to the office again today. There was something nagging at him, and he hoped to have figured out by the time she got home. Hopefully, a run and a swim would help him work it out.

"Finn?" He smiled.

"Yes?"

"It's too early to be up."

"The birds are singing."

"What time is it?"

"Seven," he answered as he went over to the bed.

"At least you're dressed for bed." He looked down and realized he was still naked, and laughed.

"Got plans for me, do you?"

"Yep."

She had held him until he had fallen asleep. She always seemed to know what he needed. He hesitated.

"You do the same for me."

"What?"

"You give me what I need too."

He looked at her in amazement. "How did you know what I was thinking?"

"Now that you're smiling, you're starting to show your emotions on your face. I've never felt so cared for in my entire life. You've done that for me."

He crawled onto the bed, and rested over her, careful not to lay his weight on top of her. "I love you, Angie." Her eyes glistened with tears.

"You do?" It said something that she questioned him.

"I do. I really do."

"Thank you."

"Ah, lady, thank you." He kissed her.

HE HAD FIGURED out what had been bothering him on mile seventeen. It seemed to be his lucky mile. He'd sent Clint an e-mail explaining everything that was going on with Dasha and the general so he would have the background on the situation prior to the call.

He picked up Angie and brought her back to the apartment with an order of Dickie's Bar-B-Que.

"What's so urgent?" she asked as they settled in front of the computer.

"I want to wait until we get Lydia and Clint on Skype."

He pressed send, then Clint and Lydia's faces filled the screen.

"Finn!" Lydia's smile almost broke her face, but the tears in her eyes almost broke his heart.

"Lydia Hidalgo and her fiancé Clint Archer, please meet Angie Donatelli."

"I've read so much about you both. It's an honor," Angie said leaning forward.

"Lean back," he admonished. "She's has a broken rib, and she needs to be careful," he explained to everyone.

"I read over everything you sent. It is absolutely unbelievable what Dasha has gone through," Lydia said.

"Isn't it?" Angie agreed.

"We have to find her baby. I mean all the mother's need to be reunited with their infants, but after I read what happened to Dasha in Odessa, I think she needs her daughter more than anyone else." Clint put his arm around Lydia.

"I think we can all agree on this, but that's not why you wanted this little pow-wow, is it, Finn?" Clint asked.

"Nope, I think eventually, Vlad is going to dig out Sergei and Lou's past relationship in the army. I think we need to get Dasha and Sergei out of Austin."

"But they feel so safe here," Angie protested.

"Angie," Finn admonished quietly.

"There are so many places we can stash them here in Austin, that they'll be safe," she suggested.

"Yeah, that's why Lorna Jackson decided to leave Austin until the trial. I'm not buying it," Finn said, dismissing her idea.

"They can come to San Diego, or they can go to Jack's parent's ranch in San Antonio," Lydia suggested.

"Both of those places are out. The general will know that the girls who were abducted have been placed in both of those areas. As a matter of fact, you need to shore up the security around those girls," Finn directed.

"Already on it," Clint clipped out.

"I'm going to call Declan and see if he has any place we can use," Finn said.

"Who's Declan?" Angie and Lydia asked simultaneously.

"You've been holding out on Lydia?" Finn asked Clint.

"It never came up," Clint grumbled. "Declan McAllister is a crap friend of Finn's who has his sticky little fingers in a lot of classified government pies. He's former Army Military Intelligence Corp. He's retired."

"So what does he do now? How is he connected to Finn? Why haven't we tapped into his resources before?" Lydia demanded.

"He's a founding member of the Shadow Alliance. He's a childhood friend of Finn's. And Finn has bounced our intelligence against Dec's in the past, but he hasn't had anything that we haven't found out on our own."

"He did feed us the information on Vlad Lutsenko because he's an international political figure. He's also got a lot of inside information on the Russian and Ukrainian mob. This is one of the cases he's going to be on the forefront for data," Finn explained.

"I call spousal foul that you haven't told me." Lydia pressed her finger into Clint's chest.

"You can't call spousal foul. We're not married. Now, if you want that privilege, you should marry me now instead of making me wait, and I'll remember to tell you every little thing."

"What's the Shadow Alliance?" Angie asked.

"It's complicated," Finn said.

"Yeah, I've never understood," Clint piped in.

"Try to explain. Is it something that's legal?" Angie persisted.

"They use their powers for good. I trust them implicitly. They might get a little fuzzy with the rules of law, but they are always on the right side of justice," Finn said.

"Sounds like people I would like," Lydia said.

Damn good thing, since Declan certainly liked her, Finn thought to himself.

"So I'll leave a message for Declan, and see what I can do to find housing for Dasha and Sergei."

"He won't answer?" Lydia asked.

"He hardly ever answers. But he always gets back to me."

HE AND ANGIE were in bed. He was sleeping soundly again when he heard the distinctive sound of an incoming Skype call. Angie muttered in her sleep, and he got up, grabbed his sweats, and closed the bedroom door as he hustled to the computer. It was Declan.

"Where the fuck are you?" He could see people all around him, men, women, and children bustling around. A child around the age of four came up, sucking her thumb, and laid her head on Declan's shoulder. He put his arm around her and cuddled her close.

"Lay off the swearing. I don't know how much English this one understands. I'm at a high school gym. We're helping set up another shelter here. It is on high ground, and should be away from the flooding, for a while, at least."

"I read up on what's going on. There are some holes you can drive trucks through. The Red Cross is getting its ass kicked."

"Instead of saving homes, we have some forces more

concerned with saving lucrative crops." Declan gave him a meaningful look. Finn got the gist of what he was saying. He knew Paraguay was one of the world's leading producers of marijuana.

"I take it your team is on it?"

"You know it." Declan's smile was savage. "But that wasn't why you called. I have a friend, former Army Ranger, who has a place on Lake Texoma."

"Alliance member?"

"Sometimes," Declan said cryptically.

"How do I get ahold of him?"

"He'll be in touch with you tomorrow. He's getting things set up." The little girl started to fall asleep, and Declan pulled her onto his lap. "Good luck, Finn. With everything. I think I know where your head's at, and know you've got a home if you want it."

"I've always known that, Dec. But I appreciate the words."

"What the hell are you talking about? I've made the offer damn near every time we've talked since I've started the Alliance."

Finn chuckled. "I look forward to hearing from your resource. What's his name?"

"Laird Campbell."

"Fuck, another Scotsman. I'm surrounded."

Declan laughed. "At least you know your girls will be safe." He cocked his head. Finn heard someone calling for him in Spanish. "I have to go."

"Thanks, Dec."

"Call me again if you need anything, including if you just need to talk."

"I will."

The screen cleared, and Finn turned around and held

out his hand. He'd heard Angie come out midway through the call.

"So that was your friend, huh?" she asked as she twined her arm around his neck and kissed the top of his head.

"Yes, that was Declan."

"Who was the little girl?"

"He's in Paraguay at a shelter for the flood victims. Kids have always been drawn to him." He pulled her down, and she slid easily into his arms. As she nuzzled his neck, he held her closer, and it settled him.

"What are the next steps?" Finn's mind had been racing since hearing about the kidnapping. It was Wednesday. He still had an appointment to keep at a strip club on Friday night.

"You and Lou are going to be driving to San Antonio tomorrow, well today" he corrected, "with Sergei and Dasha."

"I thought we would be going to Lake Texoma? I'm confused? Wait, what do you mean Pops and me, why aren't you going?" She started to get up, and he held her tighter.

"Angie, here me out," he started slowly.

Come on, Crandall, this is your strong suit, start tap dancing.

"Grace Preston's ranch is in San Antonio."

"That's south. Lake Texoma is north. Why would we go south, when we need to go north?"

"Give me a moment to explain." She vibrated beneath him.

"Okay, but make it fast, because something smells fishy."

"The four of you go down to San Antonio and acclimate Dasha to the girls who are staying with Grace. Clint didn't say it, but trust me, now that we have a plan as to where the girls are going, and we know that there might be a breach of security at the Preston Ranch, Jack Preston will be arriving there like an avenging angel."

"Then the Brady Bunch is down in San Antonio, except you are still here in Austin visiting Sixth Street. What? Is there a band playing you don't want to miss?"

"No, I'm going to be coordinating with Clint as well as checking to make sure nobody is sniffing around your granddad's house."

"I'm not buying it. Pops has security. Hell, the security feed can be routed to his phone. Try again, Finn. Why am I in San Antonio and you're in Austin? Are you even coming to Lake Texoma?"

"Of course, I'm coming to Lake Texoma. I just need a couple of days, okay, Angie? As soon as you start the trek north, I'll meet up with you, and we'll head to Oklahoma. Angie, you have to know I want to be with you."

"Well, right now it sure isn't looking like it. This is pretty suspicious. Finn, is it because you don't want to see Jack? I thought you were okay with seeing your team members again. You were fine talking to Clint on Skype."

That could work.

"I need a couple of more days before I see my teammates in person, okay?"

She placed her hands against his chest and pushed out of his lap, but her eyes never left his. She repositioned herself so she straddled him, and cupped his cheeks.

"Finn, whatever you need, I'll back you. Do you know why?"

He shook his head.

"Because I claim you. I have decided you are mine. I don't know what our future holds. There are a shit ton of obstacles. I don't know if you're going to want to claim me."

He watched her eyes fill with tears. One formed on the tip of her lash and held on for dear life.

"I know claim is such an archaic word. But my Viking, I claim you. I have seen your soul, and it is beautiful. You are brave and good, and for the rest of my life, no matter how my life plays out, I'm going to hoard our time together in the deepest recesses of my heart. I love you." The tear fell, and he licked up the salty treasure.

"You shouldn't, Angie. I'm a bad bet."

She placed the softest kiss imaginable on his lips. "You're a royal flush."

"Lady. I love you too."

"Thank you for that." Her smile could light the darkest night. She hugged him close, and they held each other for long minutes.

"I told you about my son. Now I need to tell you about Canada. I've been thinking for so long that I'm broken, but now I think maybe I can be put back together."

"Oh honey, you were never broken. There might be a few cracks, but those can be fixed, but you have never been broken."

"It's been building and building. It seems like so many innocents get hurt, and I don't get to them fast enough. They suffer. They die..." his voice drifted off.

ANGIE MADE sure she didn't wince when she sat straighter in his lap and tucked his head next to hers. This was about his pain, not hers. "Tell me," she whispered into his ear, stroking his head.

For long moments, Finn didn't say a word.

"You met Lydia. She's wonderful. God, I thought she

would die. She did. I swear Clint brought her back to life. We were too late. She shouldn't have been beaten."

He wasn't making sense. She slowly rocked him, back and forth, and he seemed to calm.

"Take your time."

"It was almost two years ago. We were late getting to a cabin where Lydia and her family were being held." He took deep gulps of air. She wrapped her arms around his head, trying to protect him, shield him from the past.

"They'd stripped and hurt her sister Beth, and Lydia sacrificed herself. She was being whipped when we got there. We killed the fuckers. She was shredded. Both of the girls were traumatized, but Lydia was sick and had been tortured. Clint carried her for five days through the jungle." He bit out the words.

"Just twenty minutes earlier. Just good fucking intel, and twenty minutes, and we would have saved her all of that pain, both girls would have been saved. They were doing CPR on Lydia when they loaded her onto the chopper."

"But she lived. She's thriving," Angie reminded him.

"But it was so close, and so often it ends in death. How many girls did the Liu's sell that we weren't able to save and who ultimately died? How many other women were killed by those bastards that had savaged Lydia and Beth? How many more people can I possibly fail?"

"But Finn, you've saved so many. I've read about the girls at the farm, you went undercover and protected them. You were one of the men on the team that saved Lydia. How can you think you fail people?" she whispered urgently into his ear. He trembled in her arms.

"I love you, Angie, I really do. But I'm no royal flush. I feel like such a failure. I'm not just sick in the head, I'm sick in the heart. I've feel like I failed everyone, and I can't take the chance that I will fail you too." He stood with her wrapped around him. He walked down the hall, both of them staring at one another.

He needed comfort. He needed to believe there was one damn person in this world that cared about him and were in his corner. He set her down on the bed and kissed her forehead. He was turning to leave when she grasped his hand.

"Angie, let me leave."

"In a moment." She brought his hand to her mouth and kissed his palm. His breath broke.

"I claimed you, Finn Crandall. You'll have to trust me to see you clearly when you can't. You're a good man. You are not a failure, you're a hero. You're my hero. I love you. You said you love me. I hope that means you like and respect me as well. You like and respect your teammates. None of us see you as a failure. We all see you as a good man. Let us be your mirror because the only thing broken about you is the reflection you see."

She watched the anguish on his face.

"Please stay with me tonight. You're sending me away in the morning. Please just let me hold you, nothing more, I'm begging you."

Maybe, just maybe, she would be able to provide him some comfort when he was feeling such unimaginable pain.

He was beside her on the bed in an instant. "Never, never do you have to beg, lady. I love you. I don't deserve you, but I need tonight. I need you."

"You have me."

11

"Pops, what the hell did you do?" Angie looked at the two hummer's parked in the driveway in the front of her grandfather's ranch house.

"I bought new cars."

Finn and Sergei smiled as they walked around the huge vehicles. Dasha looked at them with trepidation.

"When did you get these?"

"This morning. I had them delivered."

"Holy fuck!" Finn and Pop's heads whipped around to look at her. "What? I'm not allowed to swear? Just how much money did you spend? These are like military vehicles."

"Closest thing possible," her grandfather agreed. He looked at Dasha, who was sitting on one of the Adirondack chairs on the porch with her uncle.

"We're now dealing with a foreign combatant. I want the best equipment possible."

Angie closed her eyes. Then she looked at her grandfather. "Give me the key," she demanded.

"What key," he asked innocently.

"There damn well better be a key." Finn watched the

back and forth between the two Donatelli's with curiosity, but he finally caught on.

"If she's talking about what I think she's talking about. I want to see it too."

"Not in front of the girl," Pops said in a hushed tone.

"Dasha," Angie called out. "Can you get us some lemonade from the refrigerator?"

"Yes," Dasha called out. As she went into the house, Sergei immediately came down to join them.

"Lou, you going to show them your stash?"

"Yeah, Angie figured it out."

"Of course, she did," Sergei said. "Your granddaughter is no fool."

The older man opened up the back of the black hummer. He pointed to a large steel lockbox. He then handed each of them a key chain with a key fob but no key. Finn pressed the fob, and the lid to the box elevated with a hydraulic hiss.

"Well, we're ready for Armageddon," Angie said sarcastically.

Finn moved forward and pulled out one of the four assault rifles. "Four?" he asked.

"My Angela can handle one just fine," Pops said smiling proudly. Finn's head spun as he gave Angie a sharp look.

"What?" Angie asked defensively.

"Did you serve?"

"I served under Pops."

"I made sure she could handle every weapon imaginable. Hell, I fought to have her compete against boys in the 3-Gun Competition. Back then they didn't have a competition for girls."

"Pops, he doesn't need to hear about my childhood."

Angie squirmed. Finn continued to look between her and her grandfather.

"No, tell me more."

"We don't have time. We need to get on the road," she insisted.

"No we don't, Dasha is getting lemonade remember," Finn reminded her.

Pops pulled out a Sig Sauer pistol and handed it to her. It felt a little big in her hands. She handed it back to her grandfather.

"I'll stick with mine." Finn pulled out the sniper rifle and checked the balance. "Isn't that overkill?"

"I'd prefer to have too much firepower."

Crash.

Sergei immediately started talking in Ukrainian, and that was when Angie saw Dasha standing amongst broken glass and a puddle of lemonade. Finn was storing all of the weapons.

"What is this?"

"We need to be safe darlin'," Pops said.

"Why guns? What wrong?"

"Nothing's wrong," Pops soothed. Sergei attempted to put his arm around Dasha, and she shoved it off.

"No! You lie. First, we must to leave. Why? What gone wrong?" Tears rolled down her face. "Please, Angie. You tell me truth. Woman to woman. Tell me truth. I know is about my Yulia. Is my Yulia safe?"

Angie walked over to the petite young woman and took her into her arms. "The general doesn't have your baby. We are still looking for your baby," Angie assured her.

Dasha collapsed in relief, all of her weight falling onto Angie, causing her to cry out with pain. In a flash, Finn had both Dasha and Angie in each of his arms, helping both to stand.

Sergei pulled Dasha into a bear hug, and Finn held Angie's trembling form in his arms. "Let's get you sitting down." She tried to catch her breath so she could answer him, but couldn't get the words out. "Fuck this shit." He picked her up and carried her to the chairs on the porch.

Angie could still hear Ukrainian and tears behind her.

"Are you okay? Talk to me."

"I'm fine. She just took me by surprise, and hit my ribs wrong." She flashed Finn a wan smile.

"Are you sure? Do we need to rewrap the bandages? Do you need to get to the doctor?"

Angie gave him a droll stare. "You're kidding, right? Come on Finn, it was nothing, I just wasn't expecting it."

"Dammit Angie, just because everybody else thinks you can move mountains, doesn't mean it's true." Angie melted under his concern. She sat up straight in the chair and then did a slight stretch to one side and then the other.

"Seriously Finn, she didn't do any permanent damage, I'm fine."

"Okay then," he said in a mollified tone. Then he grinned. "By the way, do I call you Annie Oakley?" She buried her head in her hands.

"I would prefer you didn't. I was actually called Angie Oakley as a kid, and I hated it." She glanced at the Hummers, and the men were still there. "I hated that Pops entered me in all of those contests. But it was a way to bond with him. Mom and Dad were always busy with their own things, so I was eager to get to do a thing with my granddad, you know?"

"What is the 3-Gun Competition?"

"You have to use a rifle, shotgun, and pistol, and hit a variety of targets in a limited amount of time."

"How old were you when you started doing that?"

"Oh, I got to start when every girl dreams of shooting a gun—thirteen." She gave him a sarcastic grin. He grinned.

"Have I told you I like your smile, Crandall?" She wiped her hands on her jeans and stood up.

"Not in the last couple of hours."

"Well, you should smile more often."

He grinned.

"I guess we need to get going."

He watched as they loaded the vehicles, and then gave Angie a chaste kiss good-bye, which he immediately regretted as the cars left his sight. Dammit, he'd be happy when Paul Jackson was taken care of and he could join her.

FOR A MAN WHO WAS RETIRED, Lou Donatelli had a huge network of friends and contacts. Lou told Finn to talk to Max Jenkins, who worked at the strip club. After Finn had dropped off Angie, he stopped by the Sapphire Gentlemen's Club and spoke to Max about the illustrious Paul Jackson.

Maxine "Max" Jenkins had been very forthcoming about the bastard.

"Sure, he comes in every payday with other jerks from the mayor's office. Nine times out of ten, we have to cut Jackson off because he gets belligerent. Then he'll try to paw the girls, and one of the bouncers will bounce him. None of his *supposed* friends will lift a finger to help him. We'll call him a cab."

"What time does this normally happen?"

"Usually around midnight. I talked to Lou about having

the bouncers roughing the fucker up, but he didn't want me to do anything that might get my liquor license revoked," she said as she applied her makeup in front of the well-lit mirror.

"He's right. Letting him know where to find him is help enough."

Max looked Finn up and down. "Something tells me it's *you* knowing where he's going to be that's important. You look like someone I would turn to if I were in trouble," she flirted.

Finn looked apprehensively at one of the women headliners as well as the club owner. "I can hold my own," he agreed

"I don't suppose you might be interested in taking a job as a bouncer?"

"No. I have a job."

"A job as a boyfriend?"

"Ahhh, no?" he said nervously.

Max laughed. "Too bad. How are you connected to Lou?"

"I'm more connected to Angie."

"Dammit, I was afraid you were going to say that." But despite her words, her smile was friendly.

"Well, if it weren't for Angie, I would definitely have to say I would be sticking around for your show."

"Now aren't you gallant?"

Finn was amazed he was actually flirting. Hot damn, things were really looking up. He was beginning to enjoy life again.

"I'd appreciate it if you could keep any trouble off the premises."

"Not a problem, I'll make sure we keep your club out of it."

"I'm sure you will."

It was déjà vu all over again, only this time it was Drake Avery lounging against his El Camino.

What the fuck? At least he spotted Drake before he caught sight of him. It gave Finn a few moments to wrap his head around the fact this friend showed up just as he was headed out to bust some heads. Then again, who better to watch your back in a street fight than Drake?

"I see you up there, Crandall! Get your ass down here." Finn jogged down the steps from his apartment and made his way across the parking lot.

Before Finn could hold out his hand, Drake had him in a bear hug. "Jesus man, you look good. You've gotten laid, haven't you? Goddammit, am I the only man on this team who isn't getting any?"

Finn worried that Angie wasn't going to be the only one with broken ribs.

"Let me go, you big oaf."

"First, answer the fucking question."

"I didn't hear a question. You were busy spouting assumptions. What the hell are you doing here? Why are you here tonight?" It was pretty fucking suspicious that he was there hours before he was going to pound the shit out of Paul Jackson.

"Ah, you know how it is. Dec's been monitoring your phone calls. He heard you talking to that woman's grandfather. He tattled on you to Mason, and I'm here to make sure you don't land in jail."

Finn felt his blood pressure rise to molten lava levels.

"Dec did what? Mason did what? You made the fucking arbitrary decision I couldn't fucking handle myself? That I'm too nuts too, cope with something so simple as scaring off some little shit heel?" Finn pulled out his phone, threw it on the ground and smashed it to smithereens.

"Jesus man, touchy much?" Drake said staring at the asphalt.

Finn took a swing and stopped himself a half inch from meeting Drake's jaw. He was pissed, but bloodying up his friend wasn't going to accomplish anything.

"Good man. Let's keep all the violence channeled towards the fucker who beat up your woman." Drake grinned.

"Leave. Just get on a plane and leave."

"No."

"You go tell our lieutenant he can piss up a rope!"

"You absolute dumb son of a bitch. Like Mason would ever do what Declan tells him to do. I overheard the conversation. Mason wasn't going to do anything. He knows you're a big boy. He told Declan to 'pound sand.' Actually, I think he told him a hell of a lot more that. He was angry Dec had bugged your phone. But I could also tell he was worried about you. All in all, Mason, being the good little Boy Scout he is, and being the leader he is, was going to leave it in your hands."

"Then what are you doing here?"

"I overheard the conversation. I don't have Mason's scruples. I'm more of a Declan McAllister type of guy. So I got my happy ass on a plane. First, I wanted to give you the ration of shit you deserved for ducking out on us weeks ago in San Diego. I'm still pissed about that." Drake relaxed against Finn's car. "Second, I'm here because I thought what you were going to do was pretty fucking righteous. I wanted in on it but wanted to make sure you didn't go over the top. Not because you do or don't have Post Traumatic Stress, but because this is your woman you're defending, and he almost killed her, and you're going to have blood in your eye. I'm going to keep you from going over the edge."

Finn snorted. "Let me see if I've got this right. You, Drake Avery, are keeping me from pushing the envelope."

Drake grinned broadly. "Exactly, I'm glad you understand."

"I don't. You don't push the envelope. You tear it open. How the fuck are you going to help keep me in line?"

"See, that's where I'm the perfect guy to help. I know about your instincts to kill, and I'll be able to stop you."

It kind of made sense. "I'm still pissed at Dec being in my business."

"Cut Dec some slack, he's your family, and he's like the middle child of the family. They're sneaky, and they just can't help being who they are."

"I hate this," Finn said as he kicked the broken pieces of his phone.

"You're the one with the paranoid spy as a friend. As for hating it. Well, suck it up, buttercup. No man is an island. We're all in this together. *Kumbaya*. And whatever else I need to say to make you stop bitching. I didn't come here to listen to you whine, I came here to help you beat the hell out of some fucking redneck."

"That's rich coming from someone who talks like he's from the deep south. At least I can understand most Texans when they speak," Finn said.

"Oh give it a rest. You can understand me just fine. You're just pissed that most of the time women flock to me because of my accent."

"From now on all of the women can flock to you all they want. I've found the one I care about."

"Fuck, you too? Finn, I thought we were in this together? I thought we were going to be single forever."

"I sure as hell hope not. I don't know where this is headed with Angie, but the idea of remaining single forever doesn't hold a whole hell of a lot of appeal after meeting her."

"Damn, I guess it is just Aiden and me then."

"Guess so." Finn looked at his watch. "We better get going." Drake pushed off of the car.

"Let's take my rental truck, because apparently that's all they rent here in Texas."

Finn snorted. "I have one too. I actually got a rental pickup for the night. I figured that driving the El Camino in the area would not be smart."

"Okay, let's use that then," Drake said.

FINN HAD the man's picture blazed into his brain.

"Stop it!" Drake hit him across the chest.

"What?" Finn rounded on his friend, pissed that his concentration had been interrupted.

"You're staring a hole into him. He'll feel you, dude." Finn leaned back into the driver's seat. It was true. How many times had they felt when someone was staring, or a gun was trained on them? Prey always had a sixth sense.

"Of course, that dumb shit looks too stupid to notice. He's already drunk."

Finn nodded. He'd seen how he had stumbled out of his car on his way into to the club.

"So what's the plan? Are we going in?"

"Max called me earlier and asked me to come in. One of the bouncers would take me to the back office."

"Won't the mark notice?"

"No. I scoped out the club two days ago. It's huge, we

could have the fifth fleet come in, and nobody would notice."

"Okay, let's go."

They got out of the truck and followed a pack of young men who looked to be celebrating a bachelor party. Finn caught the eye of a man at the door and told him they were there to see Max.

"Gentlemen, follow me." He took them past the main stage, and through a small door to the right of the bar.

"Finn, it's good to see you again," Max said as she enveloped him in a hug. The woman had apparently never heard of a side hug, it was all full frontal contact.

"This is my friend, Drake." She held out her hand. Finn almost laughed, it was obvious Drake was in the mood for a chest to chest hug if his pout was anything to judge by.

"It's a pleasure, Drake."

"I take it Max is short for Maxine?" Drake asked.

"He's a smart one, good thing he has a cute ass." Drake flushed.

"I earned that one for pointing out the obvious. Now that you cut me down to size, do I get a hug?"

Max belted out a laugh.

"You get to scare the shit out of some greasy weasel, that is your prize. If you do a good enough job, come see me later, and we'll talk about your ree-ward," she said with a wink.

Drake caught her up in a quick hug. "I think I'll be getting the prize and collecting on y'alls ree-ward soon enough."

She looked up at him through her lashes, then slanted her gaze over to Finn's. "Is this boy trustworthy?" Drake gave him a pleading look.

"Not at all," Finn answered.

"Then I'm sold." Max smiled. "Here's the reason I asked you to come in. One of the regulars in there is a bailiff. He said the mayor has been trying to ensure the case gets tried by one particular judge. If Mathers hears the case, you can be damn sure that he'll swing it so Jackson doesn't see a day in prison."

Finn felt his blood boiling again.

"Then it's simple. After we're done here tonight, we go after the mayor and the judge," Drake said as he hit Max's desk with the flat of his hand.

"Hold up. I don't think Max is done telling us everything," Finn cautioned.

Max laughed. "You're right."

"Well, why didn't you say so?"

"You didn't give me enough time, cowboy."

"Apparently, Jackson has some dirt on the mayor and is forcing his hand. If you can find out what it is, maybe you can go public with it, and Jackson won't have anything to hold over the mayor's head."

"You're brilliant!" Drake pulled her into his arms again and landed a quick kiss. Then he turned to Finn. "See, now I have a girl too."

"Oh my God, you're a hot mess." She giggled. "I could learn to like you." She winked at Finn.

"Drake, flirt on your own time. We have to get out there and keep an eye on Jackson. It sounds like besides scaring the bastard, we need some information," Finn surmised.

"Sounds like," Drake agreed.

"How long are you going to be in town?" Max asked Drake.

"I have to go to San Antonio right after this."

"That's where Lou is. What's going on?" she said encompassing both men with her question.

"It's complicated," Finn answered.

"Does it have anything to do with the Ukrainian guests Lou had out at the ranch for the past six weeks?"

"How did you know about his guests?" Finn asked Max.

"Lou has been introducing Sergei and Dasha to people when he plays chess in the park. Word gets around."

Fuck! Did everyone in Austin know about Sergei and Dasha?

"Do me a favor, Max, please don't answer any questions about them if anybody comes asking, and don't mention San Antonio."

"My lips are sealed."

"Okay, let's go and see about our friend Mr. Jackson." Finn's lip curled in disgust.

He and Drake left the office, and in that little time, the number of patrons had doubled. The bouncer was waiting for them.

"Jackson's to the left of the stage with four of his friends. I have a spot saved for you behind him." He led them towards a table well back from Jackson, but they could still see him.

"I wonder if we're going to get to see Max," Drake said as he placed his drink order.

Finn continued to scan the audience and keep Paul Jackson in his peripheral vision. "Probably not based on how he's already starting to act. His friends had to pull him away from the stage, did you see that?"

Drake sighed. "Yeah."

"What?"

"I really wanted to see Max perform."

"For fuck's sake." Finn turned on Drake ready to rip him a new one when he saw the twinkle in his eye.

"You really need to loosen up, Crandall. Seriously dude. It's too easy to yank your chain."

"There he goes." Both men turned as Jackson tried to climb on stage, and another bouncer had to stop him. He turned to Paul's friends, and they all laughed and made dismissive gestures. The bouncer escorted Jackson towards the front of the club.

"I'll go first, and I'll go left," Drake said. He got up and unobtrusively made his way to the front as well. Finn gave them five minutes and then followed. By the time he made it outside they were nowhere to be seen. He went left, and a block away from the club he found them down an alley. It was dark, and Jackson was falling down drunk, it was going to be a great combination.

"Ah, here is my friend." Drake was wearing the same type of ski mask Finn had just donned.

"Please, I don't want any more trouble. Please don't hurt me anymore." Jackson was huddled against the dirty wall of the building looking at the huge Navy SEAL. It was clear that he had already put up a fight, the stupid man. Finn was pissed he allowed Drake to go first when he saw that Jackson was holding his ribs. He'd wanted to do that damage to the fucker.

"Has he told us what we needed to know?" Finn asked as he came to stand beside Drake.

"No, he hasn't." Finn hauled him up, and the man gagged in pain.

"I'll tell you anything."

Finn shoved him against the wall, pressing against his chest. Jackson screeched with agony. "Tell us why the mayor is helping you. What dirt do you have on him?"

Finn saw the indecision on his face. "If I tell you, I'll go to jail for assaulting that bitch." Finn hauled back and hit the man in the face, taking great satisfaction in watching his head bounce against the wall. He pulled back again, but before he could land a punch Drake grabbed his hand.

"Whoa, there son. We need him conscious to answer questions."

"Right," Finn agreed, shaking his head to clear it. "Answer me. What dirt do you have on the mayor?"

Jackson was crying, his nose and mouth were bleeding profusely. "He has a personal Cayman Island account where he funneled most of his Deep Black Oil campaign contributions."

"How do you know this?"

"I helped him do it." Finn patted him down, and found the man's phone, and shoved it at him.

"Give us the account number." Jackson looked at him in shock.

"I don't have it with me."

"Hit him again," Finn said to Drake. Drake pulled back his fist.

"No, I'll tell you." He fumbled with his password, and shuffled through items, then turned the phone around to show them. "This is the account." Finn went to pull out his phone to copy it and realized he didn't have one.

He could almost see Drake smirking beneath the ski mask as he tapped the numbers into *his* smartphone.

"Stay away from Angie and Lorna. We'll be watching you," Finn said as he pulled the man up by his collar and breathed into his face.

"I promise."

"I think you need just one or two more reminders." He let go of Jackson and watched dispassionately as he fell to the ground. Then he kicked him in the hip. He gave a satisfying scream.

"Are you going to bother Lorna or Angie ever again?"

188 | CAITLYN O'LEARY

"No, I promise."

Finn knew one more kick would break his hip, and as much as he wanted to do it, he knew he couldn't. He had promised himself he would just replicate Angie's beating. He kicked the man in the knee, happy when he screeched again.

"Are we done?" Drake asked.

"Nope." Finn smiled. He hauled back and kicked the man in the hip, hearing bone crunch. "Now we're done."

THEY MADE their way back to Finn's truck.

"What are we going to do with this information, oh great mastermind?" Drake asked.

"This is an election year. It's going to go to the mayor's opponent."

"I like it. I like it a lot. You're an evil bastard. I keep forgetting you grew up with Declan."

"Don't bring up his name," Finn growled. "And by the way, what's this bullshit about you going to San Antonio?" Finn demanded.

"There was this other conversation I overheard," Drake began.

"Do you spend your entire life listening in on other people's conversations?" Finn asked sarcastically.

"It's the best way to find out what the hell is going on. Also, I can find out if someone is talking behind my back. They often are. Some people are under the mistaken impression that I speak before I think. I don't know where they have gotten this idea. I'm always thinking. Hell, I'm the idea man of this team."

Finn choked out a laugh.

"Don't even, it's true. How often have we been in a tight situation, and I have come up with some counterintuitive solution?"

Finn thought about it and realized it was true.

"But still, you're listening at doorways."

"All part of being a smart man, and coming up with the plans, my boy. You should try it some time. That's why I like your man Declan so much. If I knew how to tap into all of your cell phones, I would be doing that twenty-four seven."

"You are such an asshole."

"At least I'm up front about it."

"So who did you listen into to find out about San Antonio?"

"Jack. As soon as Clint told him that his ranch might be overrun by the Ukrainian Special Forces looking for Dasha, the man was ready to defend it like the Alamo. He spoke to his stepdad, and brother. Apparently, they have a fucking army of ranch hands. But he's going to go and coordinate things."

"Is he taking Beth?"

"He sure as hell doesn't intend to. But three bucks says in her quiet, determined way, she manages to talk him into going. That girl has a spine of steel."

"So he's going to be in San Antonio with his mom and the displaced girls. He's not planning on going with us to Lake Texoma, is he?"

"He didn't mention it."

"Did you even talk to him about this?"

"Nope, I heard both conversations the same day, and figured I would just go with the flow when I got to Austin."

Drake was kind of making Finn's head hurt.

12

THE FAMILIAR SOUND OF THE SKYPE INCOMING CALL RANG AT five in the morning. Finn was already awake, and contemplating making coffee. Even though it had been a late night, he was anxious to make the hour drive to San Antonio. He and Drake both made it to the computer at the same time.

Angie was on the screen, she looked frantic.

"You're okay! Oh God, you're okay. Thank God." Then she burst into tears. Jack was beside her.

What the fuck?

"Jack, what's going on?" Finn demanded.

"There was an explosion at her grandfather's ranch. She couldn't reach you on your cell phone." There was nothing left to say, Finn connected the dots.

"You bastard! Why didn't you answer your phone?" She wiped her nose and glared at him.

"He–" Drake started to say something.

"Shut it." Finn elbowed his friend.

"When did the explosion take place?" Finn leaned forward and demanded.

"A half hour ago. Pops was alerted on his phone's security system. He wants to drive up, but Jack won't let him."

"Good man," Finn praised Jack.

"Finn, he keeps horses," Angie explained tearfully.

"We're going over there now. Jack, as soon as I check on the damage, I'll be heading on down to San Antonio. Have everybody ready to leave."

Jack nodded, his eyes clear and alert.

"We." Finn turned to Drake and sighed.

"We," he said.

"What's Avery doing there with you?" Jack asked.

"It's a long story," Finn said shaking his head at Jack. He didn't want to take the time to explain.

"Finn?" Angie asked.

"Yes, honey?"

"You'll be careful when you go to the ranch, won't you?" She touched the computer screen, he could almost feel her caressing him.

"Always," he promised.

"I'll keep him safe," Drake chimed in.

"Who are, oh never mind. Just be safe Finn," she said wearily. The fact Angie's normal curiosity was gone told him just how badly this was affecting her.

"I'll be in San Antonio soon. Just hold on for me, okay lady?"

"I'll try, but I worry for Pops."

"Where is he?" Finn asked. When Angie didn't answer, he turned to Jack.

"He's with my mom," Jack answered.

"I'll see you soon, Angie."

The connection went dead.

"She's gorgeous," Drake said as he got up from the table. Both men were heading to their respective bedrooms at a run. Finn came out dressed and packed and was waiting for Drake.

"Hurry up," he yelled.

Drake came out still stuffing things into his duffel.

"We're taking your rental truck," Finn told Drake.

"Okay. Tell me which way to the ranch."

"No need, I'm driving. Hand over the keys. I want to get to the ranch in one piece."

"Oh ye of little faith," Drake said as he handed over the keys.

Finn made the trip in record time. From miles away, they could see the plume of smoke.

Firemen were at the scene, and it was cordoned off.

"I'm Lou Donatelli's son-in-law," Finn lied easily. "He called me and wanted me to check on the horses."

"The horses are fine, just jittery. Maybe you can help get them calmed down. Let me take you to the stables. This was definitely arson. Do you know someone named Dasha?" the fire marshal asked.

On the side of the stable, painted in huge letters, was *Give Me Dasha*. Finn's step faltered, but then he kept going into the structure. He could hear the horses stamping their feet.

A truck pulled up. Soon another man was in the barn with him and Drake.

"Hey, my name is Herb. I'm Lou's neighbor on the north. I brought a horse trailer. I figured I would board, Willow and Lefty until Lou rebuilds." Finn looked at the man gratefully.

"I'm Finn Crandall, this is my friend Drake Avery."

"Is this about Dasha?" Herb asked. "I saw the writing on

the stable. She's a pretty young thing. I really like her uncle. He served."

"Yes, it is about Dasha. If you could keep it under your hat right now, even from the fire marshal, I'd appreciate it. We're handling it with Lou. Dasha's in trouble."

"I figured that much. Holler if I can help."

"Will do. We're going to meet up with Lou now."

"Where is he?" Herb asked.

"He and Angie are staying with some friends."

"Gotchya. I'll keep my mouth shut."

Finn liked these Texans, they knew how to handle a crisis.

"You think he has a target on the others," Drake said.

"I think we need to get the fuck out of San Antonio as fast as possible. They are too fucking close."

"You know they probably found them through the Sergei and Lou connection." Drake reminded Finn.

"If the general has ties to the Ukrainian Embassy, he has ties to our government. The baby ring is known to the government."

"But still, it's been our team that placed the girls, and we've kept it on the down-low," Drake insisted.

"Think Drake. They left that demand for Dasha. They had to have something to back it up. What else do they have? They're coming after the girls."

"Let's call Clint," Drake said already dialing.

"After that, I want to call Declan. I'm sick of waiting around for the general to get in touch with us. It's about time we get in touch with him. I might have an idea."

IT WAS STRUCTURED madness when they got to the ranch. Drake won the bet. Beth Hidalgo was there with Jack Preston, and that was part of the problem. She and her soon-to-be mother-in-law were in the great room, explaining in very sweet terms why it would be beneficial for the two of them to go to Lake Texoma with the young women. Jack was sweating bullets. Where in the hell were Jack's father and brother?

Finn pulled Angie aside. "Where are the girls?"

"They're upstairs. Rosa is keeping them there while the debate is going on." Finn remembered that Rosa was the Preston's housekeeper.

"What about Jack's dad and brother?"

"He called them. They left early to check out one of the outer perimeters. They're heading back now."

"Damn, his mother planned this, didn't she?"

"Oh yeah, she's diabolical." Angie sounded so tired.

"How are you holding up?"

"Better than Pops."

"Where is he?"

"With Sergei. He's sitting in the kitchen in a daze."

Angie and Finn walked back to where they were all standing. Finn wasn't surprised to see Drake standing beside Jack.

"Jack, you know the girls have been with me for over a month. They'll feel safer if I'm with them," Grace was explaining.

"Beth, I understand Mom's position, why do you think you should come?" Beth looked calmly between Grace and Jack.

"I've been in their shoes. I was taken by men intent on

selling me. They're still trying to heal from their experiences, and I might not have worked with these girls, but I've been helping the girls in San Diego, and I know I can help these girls." Finn saw Jack waver. Damn, Beth sure knew how to play him. Actually, both women did.

"Enough! We're going into a war. They just blew up Angie's grandfather's ranch. You want us to put the two of you at risk? Are you out of your fucking minds? Pardon me, ma'am. We need two more civilians at risk like we need to drag around fucking anchors! Pardon me, ma'am. Your husband would string Jack up by his fucking balls if he let you go! Pardon me, ma'am."

"I don't know who this man is Grace, but I tend to agree with him." Everybody turned to see Richard Preston crossing the foyer into the great room. He looked grim as he reached his wife and put his arm around her waist. "Just what trouble are you stirring up?"

"Man, she wants to do the craziest shit you wouldn't believe—"

"Drake, we've heard enough from you," Jack said tiredly. "Hi, Dad. Your timing is perfect as always."

"Want to explain things to me?"

"I was trying to logically explain to Beth and Mom why going to Lake Texoma was a bad idea."

"Actually, we were just being told, by Drake Avery, isn't it?" Grace asked.

"I'm sorry, ma'am. Yes, my name is Drake Avery." He flushed. She pulled away from her husband and held out her hand, and he gave it a gentle shake.

"As I was saying, I think Drake did an exemplary job of explaining why it would behoove us to stay here at the ranch, even if his delivery left something to be desired." Finn smacked Drake on the back of the head.

"Would I really be an anchor?" Beth asked Jack.

"I'd be worried about you twenty-four/seven, instead of focused on my job. So yeah, you would hold me back. I'm sorry, honey." She put her arms around him.

"There's nothing to be sorry for," she said placing a gentle kiss on his lips. Finn's arm tightened around Angie.

She gripped his hand where it rested against her tummy and looked up at him. "I like your friends."

Grace and Beth looked at one another. "We better go get the girls," Beth said to Grace.

"That would be much appreciated," Jack said in a soft drawl.

Finn saw Drake turn and zero in on them. "Oh fuck, Drake's headed this way. Maybe you should go upstairs with Beth and Grace."

"Don't be silly."

Drake came over and pulled Angie out of Finn's arms, and pulled her into a gentle hug before Finn had a chance to warn him to be careful. "Angela Donatelli, you are a hero, you got this man to pull the stick out of his ass. We, the members of Midnight Delta, will be forever grateful."

"Don't be an asshole," Angie pushed out of Drake's arms. "Finn is a great guy, and he did not have a stick up his ass. If you are actually a friend of his, you wouldn't talk shit about him." She stood toe to toe with the big man, spitting like a kitten against a Rottweiler.

"Hey, I didn't mean anything bad by it. I'm just saying Finn is doing better since meeting you. You've been a good influence on him."

Angie was slightly mollified by that statement. "Well okay then." Seeing her in her capris and a short sleeved blue shirt, with her abundant curls, and securely planted in his corner, was making him hot and bothered. Drake looked over the top of Angie's head and pointedly at his crotch and grinned. Finn flipped him the bird.

"Angie, I want to welcome you to the family."

"The family?"

"Midnight Delta. We're a family. You mean a lot to Finn. Wherever this goes, you are always going to special to us, and if you ever need anything, you just call us."

Angie's head whipped around to look at Finn. "Is he for real?"

"He's dead serious."

"You do this for all your girlfriends?"

"You're a hell of a lot more than my girlfriend." She stared at him, her brown eyes searching his. Just as she was about to ask another question the girls came down the stairs.

DID FINN really mean what she thought he meant? Her deepest dream had always been for a man like Finn to want her. Somebody strong and loving that she could depend on to return her love and not abandon her. Was it possible Finn Crandall would finally be the person who would love her unconditionally?

"Hello, Mr. Crandall." She watched as Finn blanched and sweat formed on his brow.

Angie and Finn turned to see the pretty girl who stood next to Grace. She couldn't be more than eighteen.

Angie saw Finn swallow and his mouth open, but no words came out. Drake spoke, "Hi Penny. You're looking good."

"Thank you, Drake." She gave a broad grin and picked at

the pink blouse on top of her jeans. "Grace bought this for me."

"Hello, Penelope," Finn finally croaked out. Angie sidled up beside him and wrapped an arm around him. He was soaked with sweat and trembling. This must be the girl from the farmhouse.

Penelope looked sideways at Grace, who nodded at her. She looked at Finn. "I wanted to say thank you."

"For what? I hurt you," he said harshly.

She looked at him quizzically. "You didn't. You saved me."

Finn's trembling increased. "I didn't. I hurt you. I held you down." Grace gasped. Drake walked around, and stood on the other side of Finn, and put a supportive hand on his shoulder.

"What are you talking about, buddy?"

"When they poured hot sauce down her throat, I held her down," he said in an anguished voice.

Penelope set her hand on his chest. "No, you saved me. Those men were going to rape me. You stopped them. You saved me, Mr. Crandall. You saved me."

"No! I hurt you." Angie watched in horror and relief as tears started to fall down his face.

Penelope was not put off by his display of emotion, she patted his chest. "No, you saved me," she argued. "You protected me."

"I held you down."

"You made sure all of us were safe," she reassured him. "You did the right things."

Drake's arm snaked around Finn's waist, and they were both supporting Finn.

"I should have stopped them." Angie ached for him, it was clear this had been killing him.

"You would have blown the mission, Finn," Drake said.

"No!" He shouted. "I should have figured out a way."

"You kept us safe. I am alive. I am well. I am happy today, because of you. I thank you, Mr. Crandall." Finn crumpled. Drake took all of his weight, but Angie was there to comfort him. Penelope seemed to understand, she took a step backward and she and Grace walked away.

"I don't understand."

Angie jerked her head to a chair in the corner of the room. Drake helped guide Finn to the chair. Peripherally she saw Jack and his father getting all of the girl's bags outside to the vehicles. As soon as Finn was settled into the chair, she squatted in front of him, but he clasped her wrist and pulled her into his lap.

He was beginning to get color back into his face.

"You must be doing better if you have the good sense to cuddle with this beauty."

"Fuck off, Drake, and go help load the car." Finn sighed.

"You're not going to freak out or anything, are you?"

Angie glared at the big man. Apparently, he had no sense whatsoever.

"Fuck off, Drake. Any freak-outs will be directed solely at you."

"I'm looking forward to it." Drake sauntered off.

"I'm sorry you had to see that," Finn said as he settled Angie more comfortably in his arms.

"Great, I get to have a panic attack in a parking garage, but you can't lose it in front of me? In that case, this is never going to work." Angie didn't really mean it. She was just trying to make a point.

Finn realized what she was doing because he gave a slight smile. "I can't believe she has forgiven me," Finn said in amazement.

"She hasn't. She said there wasn't anything to forgive. There's a difference." Angie cupped his cheek and delivered the softest kiss she could to his lips. She tasted salt, and her heart ached for him. All the pain he had stored up; all the anger he had been directing at himself was unimaginable.

"There was another girl. Her name was Liliya. I don't think she was even sixteen. She offered to go down on me if I would just let her go. I felt like a monster," he told her as his voice shook. She'd never seen his eyes so dark.

"Is she safe now?"

"Yes," he said slowly. "She's back home now."

"You know you did nothing wrong, don't you?"

"Sometimes my head does, but my heart hasn't gotten the message." Angie nodded. It was the same with her cousin Bruno when he'd gotten back from Iraq. And not just with him. It was the same with her. She rationally knew her parents loved her, but her heart still hurt when they didn't come and see her in a shooting tournament because they were off playing bridge.

"I wish I could wave a magic wand and make you see that all of this isn't all your fault. I love you, Finn Crandall. You're the best man I have ever met. Your team loves and respects you because you're worthy. Even that oaf, Drake, thinks the world of you, you can tell. It's because *you're a good man, and you're worthy.*" She hesitated.

"Lady, just say it."

"I think you need some help."

He sighed. "I think I do too. This all swirls around like a tornado, and I can't seem to get past it. It hurts so badly. You seem to keep it at bay, but asking you to be my security blanket isn't fair to you."

This time, she forced herself up so she was looking

directly at him. "I'll be your security blanket for as long as you need me. You've become my blanket too."

"Oh, Angie."

"Let's get a move on. Westward Ho," Drake called from the doorway.

"I hate him," Finn said.

"No you don't, you love him."

"Nope, I *hove* him. It's a combination of hate and love."

"I thought I would die when he was swearing at Grace." Angie giggled.

"Oh, he totally regretted it afterwards, I could tell. But he gets on a roll, and his mouth takes over his brain. He'll be sending her flowers, mark my words."

Angie giggled again.

"Seriously, move your asses," Drake yelled.

As SOON AS they got outside, Lou was waiting for them, his face ashen. He motioned them away from the vehicles and held out his cell phone.

"I hadn't checked my messages since the explosion. This is all my fault."

"Pops, what is it?" Angie demanded.

"Listen." He put his phone on speaker and pressed play.

Give us Dasha, if you don't, the Preston Ranch is next.

"Jack!" Finn yelled.

Jack came at a run along with his brother and father.

Lou played the message again.

"Over my dead body." Richard Preston said.

"I'm not going to Texoma," Jack said.

"Of course," Finn agreed.

"David, fire up the helicopter. Beth and your mother are

out of here now. No packing purses only. They're going to the condo in Dallas." Richard said.

David ran to the house.

"Dad, what about you? You're going to leave too, aren't you?" Jack asked.

"Not a chance in hell. Were you planning to?"

"No, Mom and Beth can go with David, I was hoping you would too," Jack said. His father just looked at him. "Fine, Jack relented. We'll both stay here, there's not a fucking chance in hell they're going to blow up this ranch."

"That's my boy." The men smiled at one another, in perfect accord.

Out of the corner of his eye, Finn saw Drake pocketing his phone.

"Who did you call?"

"Mason."

"What for?"

"If Jack isn't going with us to Texoma, I want another person on our six." Finn nodded in agreement.

He turned to Angie and Lou. "Okay, let's get going."

13

"WHAT THE FUCK KIND OF PLACE IS THIS? IT LOOKS LIKE SOME kind of compound. Does he have a bunch of sister wives?"

"Goddammit Drake, do you ever not say the first thing that pops into your head?" Finn asked as he hit his head on the steering wheel.

"What's a sister wife?" Penelope asked from the backseat.

"Why don't you answer that question, Drake."

"Never mind, I was talking out my ass, Penny."

Finn made it through the fence topped with barbed wire.

"Shit, is that a guard tower?" Drake asked.

"Looks like." Finn peered at the people in the backseat. He caught Angie's eye. She raised an eyebrow. He shrugged his shoulders. As they made it up the drive, they saw smaller cabins and then a huge log cabin that looked like something out of Architectural Digest.

"Damn, just how much money does this dude have?" Drake asked no one in particular.

A big man with auburn hair came out onto the front

steps and watched them come up the driveway. He did not look very welcoming. Since Finn was driving the lead Hummer, he decided to get out first and talk to Campbell.

"Hello, thanks for agreeing to let us stay at your place."

"It sounds like we might eventually have a war on our hands." Hard amber eyes assessed Finn.

"I think it's possible."

"I look forward to it. How many noncombatants do we have?"

"Four, but we have two marines from the Vietnam era, they are strong in spirit, I'm not sure how strong in body they will be."

"How many men?"

"We have two SEALs right now. My woman is trained, she'll be an asset. My lieutenant will be here shortly."

"Good. Let's get the innocents into the main house ASAP, then we can have a briefing. Anyone who has been a marine will always be a marine." Finn nodded, he liked the man.

Finn and Laird jogged down the stairs and helped unload the vehicles. They made quick work of getting the girls into their rooms upstairs.

"Penelope, can you and the girls start dinner," Angie asked.

"Yes."

"Let me show you where everything is," Laird said as he started towards the kitchen. Penelope put her hand on his arm.

"If it is a kitchen, we can manage," she assured him.

He assessed her, then nodded. "Just give me a shout if you need anything." He pointed to a room. "We'll be in my office." He motioned for the others to follow him. Finn put his hand on the small of Angie's back and guided her toward the office.

"Mason is going to be here in twenty minutes," Drake said, looking at his watch. "Campbell, are you one of those survivalists?"

"I bought this place from one of those survivalists. It suits my needs. Don't look a gift horse in the mouth." There was a high pitched beep that sounded.

"I guess your man has arrived sooner than you thought." Laird went behind his desk to a computer and tapped in a code. A huge monitor appeared on the wall. They could clearly see a car with Mason in the driver's seat. "I can activate the gate from the computer, the panel at the door, or from my watch. I'll get you all the codes." He clicked in a code and the gates opened.

"I'll go meet Mason and bring him in," Finn said.

"Did they have like sister wives and shit?" Drake asked as he left the room. He opened the door as Mason was getting ready to knock. God, it was good to see his boss. Mason looked tired and grim.

"Dammit, Finn, I was hoping to see you under better circumstances."

"So was I."

Mason gave a half smile. "You're looking better than when I last saw you, though. We've missed you." Mason put both hands on Finn's shoulders and looked into his eyes. "I've missed you. Are you doing okay?"

"It gets better every day, but no, I'm not there yet."

"Better is good. Better is damn good." The tension around Mason's eyes eased. "What kind of place did Declan manage to find for us? And where is everybody?"

"The girls are making dinner. Angie and the men are in Laird's office. Before we go in there, I wanted to let you know

I have an idea I want to run by the team. It might seem out there." He hated that he was even the slightest bit hesitant.

"If you have an idea, then I sure as fuck want to hear it," Mason said decisively.

"Okay, let's go."

Finn pushed the office door open, and Laird turned from the screen where he was pointing out the layout of the compound.

"Mason Gault. I've heard about you. It's a pleasure."

"Laird Campbell. The same." Mason moved forward and shook Laird's hand. "You worked with our Captain Hale on a mission. He mentioned you a couple of times in passing."

"Telling tales out of school, huh? Well, he sang your team's praises. When Declan called, I was happy to help out."

Mason frowned. "Yeah, well I'm not too happy with Declan at the moment."

"It ebbs and flows with him. We're just going over the footprint of the compound. Declan said he will have the general's private number tonight."

"What are you talking about?" Mason asked.

"That's part of the plan I was talking about," Finn said.

Everybody turned to look at him. "The general has been finding us, but it's time for us to set up the trap."

"You're thinking here. This place would be a good spot," Laird said thoughtfully.

"How would you get him to come to this place, just say, 'hey, here we are'?" Drake asked sarcastically.

"Shut it down, Avery," Mason clipped out. "Continue," he said to Finn.

"I'm not quite sure. We get them to figure out our location. Either through the back and forth communication when we call the general, or when they demand to see Dasha. Which you know they will."

"Shit, that could work," Drake said excitedly.

"We need to call Clint. He needs to figure out how to do this, so it doesn't look like we're leaving breadcrumbs. It needs to look like we were trying to hide our location," Mason said thoughtfully.

Finn liked this more and more. Angie stepped over to him and squeezed his hand. He returned the squeeze and caught Mason's glance. Nothing ever escaped Mason's notice.

DECLAN'S CALL came two hours after a subdued dinner. Between Lou's sorrow over losing his ranch and Dasha's torment about her baby, even Drake couldn't raise the energy.

Laird motioned for the team to meet him in his office while the girls cleaned up. "Hey everyone, I have Clint on the line. We've been discussing how we can dink with the general's phone, e-mail, or Skype." Declan's distinctive voice came through the phone.

"Do you have the phone number we need?" Mason asked.

"Yes. I gave Vlad's number to Clint. He should be able to call it and at least track it to the nearest cell phone tower unless he has it encrypted, which is very well possible."

"Thank you, McAllister," Mason said.

"You're welcome. I'm going to have my phone on me for the next two days, I'll answer if any of you call."

"I appreciate it," Mason responded.

"He hung up," Clint said.

"Hey Clint, it's Finn. I want to run an idea by you. Is there any way we can arrange it so these bastards can track us here?"

"You want them to come to you? You want to bait a trap, is that it?" Clint asked.

"Do you have a plan for the girls?" Mason asked.

"There's a safe room. Hell, it's not a room, it takes up half of the basement," Drake explained.

"Are we good now?" Clint asked over the phone.

"Yep," Finn answered. "And yes, in answer to your question. We want to bait a trap. How do we do it?"

"We can't do it by the phone call. We would have to do it via the internet. Do you think you could get him to do some kind of Skype call or e-mail with you?"

"If that's what we need to do, then that's what we'll do," Finn said vehemently. "But we need to do it in such a way, that it doesn't look too easy. We need to make them work for it."

"I can ping them around the world, but still, end up finding you."

"Perfect." Finn grinned. His team was the best in the world.

"How soon do you need to set this up?"

"What e-mail or Skype address are you going to use?" Finn looked at Mason, who nodded. "Mason's," Finn answered.

"Give me an hour, then call your general. We'll still try to trace his phone. There's still the possibility that he doesn't have his location encrypted."

Finn snorted, "Yeah, I'll hold my breath."

IT HAD BEEN DECIDED that Sergei would make a brief call to the general, and demand he call Mason's Skype number if he wanted Dasha, and would call off the attacks. Three minutes after Sergei hung up the call to come in, but the general didn't do a video feed. He immediately started speaking in Ukrainian.

Earlier Angie had overheard Mason and Finn talking in the hall. Finn's lieutenant had said since Finn had been on point for this whole operation, it made sense for him to continue to take the lead. The confidence Mason had in Finn was tangible, and it warmed Angie's heart. Therefore, it was Finn who interrupted General Vlad Lutsenko's tirade.

"General, I don't know what you're saying, nor do I care."

"What is it you want? Why have you demanded this call? Who is Dasha?" the man said in heavily accented English.

"Cut the shit. If you want Dasha, you'll start negotiating now."

"I don't understand. Negotiating for what. Who is this Dasha?"

"The girl whose boyfriend you killed. The girl who you are threatening to blow up half of Texas to find." Finn said with barely suppressed rage.

"I am a high ranking officer of the Ukraine. I will notify your government of your slander."

"Go ahead."

"I don't know what you're talking about. You are accusing me of some kind of crime, and I will not have it."

"Fine, then we have nothing to talk about."

"Wait, don't hang up." Everybody in the room grinned. They had the general just where they wanted him. He was stalling for time. He must be trying to trace the call.

"I cannot comment on this on an unsecure line, you must understand," the man wheedled.

"I don't have time for your bullshit," Finn bit out.

"You must allow me to investigate what you are saying."

"Dasha Koval. Does that name ring a bell? You know her from Odessa." The screen went blank. The general had hung up.

Angie felt a surge of excitement. Another call came through, this time, it was Clint and Lydia whose faces came onto the screen.

"Austin. We were able to trace him back to Austin. We weren't able to pinpoint his exact location, but his IP address was definitely Austin," Lydia said excitedly.

"Will he be able to locate us?"

"Yes. I arranged it," Clint promised.

"It sounds like we have six hours before they'll be here," Laird said. "I think we all need to get some rest." Angie was on board with that plan. She was tired, and she hurt, and she wanted to rest in Finn's arms.

"Maybe we'll have six hours," Mason said thoughtfully. "I hate taking things for granted."

"You're right," Laird agreed. "I'll take first watch."

"I'll relieve you in two hours," Mason said.

Angie looked at her grandfather, who for the first time was beginning to look his age. She started to go to him, but he waved her off.

"I think I'm going to have a drink with Sergei, and talk over old times. You go rest, honey."

"No, I need to go check on the girls." Angie started towards the stairs.

"Penelope took cocoa upstairs to the girls an hour ago. She has everything under control," Sergei assured her.

"But I should say goodnight."

"They're probably already asleep," Sergei assured her.

"Are you sure?" Angie didn't want to sound too anxious, but Sergei gave a knowing chuckle anyway.

"Yes. You and your man go to bed," her grandfather finally ended the discussion. She grinned.

Finn was huddled up with the other men of his team, but at her grandfather's words, he excused himself. He came over to her and put his arm around her. "Laird said we can have one of the cabins."

"You mean one of the sister wives houses?" Angie teased.

"I don't care what it is, as long as it affords us some privacy." They snagged their stuff from the hallway, before heading out the front door and down the steps.

The night was clear and beautiful. The sky filled with stars. As soon as the cabin door shut behind them, she turned to Finn. "Are you all right? I know today has been stressful."

He stared at her, his eyes deep and solemn.

"What?" she asked. He cupped the back of her neck and pulled her close. "What Finn? What is it? Are you all right?" He had to be all right. She needed him to be all right. He was her rock. He had to be steady. He had to be strong.

"Let it out, baby."

"No. I'm okay. I'm worried about you," she insisted.

His thumb traced circles on the nape of her neck. "Let it out," he whispered. "I'm so sorry about your grandfather's ranch."

Oh God. The ranch. She practically grew up on that ranch, the bluebonnets, the ridge, the range. She grabbed at the front of his shirt, and her breath hitched. She swallowed. She needed to control herself. She needed to get past this. Nobody liked a whiner.

"I've got you, Angie. It's okay, baby. I'm here for you."

She looked into his eyes. This man who had been

through so much. Who had lost so much. Yet he was here for her, and she could break on his shore. Angie let loose and started to cry. Big gulping ugly sobs, not just for the ranch, but for so much more. For all the times she hadn't been allowed to cry because there hadn't been someone to hold her, someone to offer solace, comfort, love, and tell her it was okay to need.

He swung her into his arms and took her to the too small bed that would be perfect to press close to Finn. She didn't want a sliver of space between them as he sheltered her through the hours before dawn. Never once in the long minutes of her weeping did he tell her to stop, he just held her and kissed her and told her he was there for her and he loved her. Everything he did was like sunlight to a new rose. It helped her grow and flourish.

"I love you too, Finn."

He kissed the top of her head. "I don't deserve you."

"I think we're both pretty lucky to have found one another. Now if we can survive the zombie apocalypse we can start talking about a future."

"I want a future with you." He tipped her chin up so he could see her face. "I want it very badly. I want you to go into the safe room with the girls. Please, Angie. You're still not healed."

"We don't know how many are coming. You'll need me."

"We have a good idea. Declan said there are ten men who always travel with the general. You can be damn sure he won't be here. So we shouldn't have more than ten."

"They could have hired some mercenaries."

"This isn't something they would outsource."

Angie gave a weak laugh.

"What?"

"I have been dreaming for a strong, protective man to

love me. Now I finally get one, and I'm pissed because he wants to put me in the safe room. Well, Finn, you knew what you were getting too, and it wasn't the shy retiring type who would be going into hiding. So, thank God we love each other for who we really are."

She saw him mulling over her point, and he didn't laugh. He pulled her even closer. "If something happens to you, I won't be able to survive it."

"I'll be careful. This isn't my first rodeo."

"I know, but your last rodeo didn't go so well."

"It was an ambush. This time, we're ready for them. Hell, Laird has landmines. I could learn to love him," she said.

Finn huffed out a laugh. "The guy is something else. He *is* actually ready for the zombie apocalypse."

She stroked her hands up the front of his T-Shirt and kissed his throat. She reveled in his groan.

"Angie, you need your rest."

"I need this more."

He clasped her wrists in one big hand. "I'm serious, we need to sleep."

"Seriously, are you going to sleep, or doze with one eye open?" She watched him. It was a 'gotchya,' as he flushed. She shook her hands out of his grasp and cupped his face. "Make love to me."

"Always. It will always be lovemaking." Then he grinned down at her. "Well except for the times when we get to down and dirty fucking."

She burst out laughing. "Oh cowboy, I can't wait. Can we do that now?" she asked eagerly, her legs rubbing together.

"I think the lady will be satisfied." His hand cupped her breast and squeezed, his thumb rubbed against her nipple, and made her moan.

She slapped her hand over his, pressing down. "Harder."

His mouth slammed down on hers, she opened, her head spun as the sexy thrusts of his tongue matched the timing of his leg scissoring between her thighs. Her head was about to explode. He unbuttoned her blouse and then unclasped her bra. Soon the feel of his calloused hands caressing her breasts was sending her into the stratosphere. She gasped, and his head reared back.

"Angie," he said thickly. She looked into storm blue eyes. "Am I hurting you?"

"Only if you stop."

He lifted her up, and stripped off her top and bra, leaving her in the Capri pants.

"Let me get up. I want out of my clothes. I want *you* out of *your* clothes." She saw him looking at her bandage. "If you obsess about my ribs one more time, I won't lick your cock."

14

Could there be a more perfect woman than Angie Donatelli? She made him laugh, she could make him lose his mind in bed, and she was a true partner.

"I was staring at your breasts." Which was partly true.

"Oh, well that's acceptable," she conceded, her eyes twinkling.

He helped her out of the bed and knelt in front of her.

"What are you doing?"

"Helping you out of your clothes." He unbuttoned her Capris, slowly pulling her pants and panties down her body. She was his ideal. She braced herself on his shoulders and stepped out of her clothes.

She was wet, he could see moisture glistening on her folds. It was too tempting to resist, he leaned forward and tasted.

"Finn," she wailed. He continued to lick and torment, holding her upright, then she folded on top of him. "It's too much." He lifted her to the bed. Angie melted onto the comforter. He quickly stripped as she watched him through hooded lids. She smiled when he pulled a condom out of his wallet.

"I love how you look."

"That's my line," he responded.

"No seriously. I see you, and I get aroused." She moved her hands down her body and parted her legs. "See?"

She was going to give him a heart attack. "Yeah, I see." He crawled onto the foot of the bed and parted her legs even further. He continued his play where he had left off, loving how Angie responded. She enjoyed every moment, thrusting upwards.

"More. Your fingers. Your cock."

He thrust two fingers inside her tight, wet sheath, and gloried at the way she shivered and begged for more. He caressed that spot at the top of her channel. She trembled, and he suckled her clit, making her pussy clench as she shouted her release. He waited until she calmed, and then started all over again.

"No, it's too much."

"One more," he coaxed. He could drown in her pleasure. Her shudders began again, and her feet and shoulders were the only things touching the bed. She screamed his name as she came again.

He couldn't roll on the condom fast enough. He plunged in as her sheath still quivered.

"Oh God, yes." At this rate, he wouldn't have to thrust as her pussy clutched around him. But soon he was driving in and out, and she was begging for more. He wasn't going to last much longer, and he was damned if she wasn't going to go with him. He kept his balance on one arm and moved his other between their bodies until he found her engorged clit.

"Oh, oh, please." He circled it softly, as he surged up and

up. She let out a shriek he thought was his name and clamped down on him. He lost his mind, his body, his soul.

———————

FOUR HOURS later he walked out of the cabin and found Drake and Mason. They turned as he walked towards them, and they had the same shit eating grin on their faces.

Drake was smoking a cigar, and he offered him one.

"Jesus, when did you start smoking?" Finn asked.

"I do it when I'm celebrating. You know, weddings, babies, friends who get their shit together."

"Fuck you, Avery." It felt good to be around his team again. "So I'm not the only one who can't sleep?"

"There's just too many variables. I don't trust that they're all coming from Austin. They could get here sooner," Mason said. "Sleep is overrated. Drake decided to join me on watch."

"Didn't stop Finn from taking a nap," Drake said. Putting air quotes around the word nap.

"Cut the guy some slack, you're just jealous," Mason said.

"No, I'm not. I found the love of my life back in Austin. She's an entertainer named Maxine." Finn rolled his eyes. "She asked for my number and everything."

"No, she said she *had* your number."

"Same difference. She intends to call me and have her wicked way with me." They laughed, and then stood in companionable silence for a while.

"I like the old man, it's a shame about his ranch," Drake said as he put out his cigar.

"From everything I've come to know about him, he'd take Sergei and Dasha in again in a heartbeat," Finn said.

He thought about the poor girl and all she had been through. Then he thought about her daughter. It shouldn't be much longer now that they had her location narrowed down to Indianapolis, but he wouldn't be happy until he saw them together.

"Quit with the dark thoughts. We agreed those were a thing of the past, now that you're in love." Drake clapped Finn's shoulder.

Finn shrugged. "I'm working on it."

"Drake, cut it out. There's a whole hell of a lot of things up in the air. If you tell me to start shitting rainbows, I'll cut you. Now's the time to have our head in the game." Mason told his second in command.

"You guys need to learn to take life as it comes. Right now, it's a nice night. We need to concentrate on that."

"Do you hear that?" Mason asked as he cocked his head. "Fuck, it's a helicopter. Move men." They immediately dispersed. No talking was necessary. They each knew their role. Finn bolted towards the cabin where Angie was, but before he could get to the front door, it was open, she was dressed and holding her gun.

"Helicopters," they said simultaneously.

"I'll make sure Pops and Sergei are awake." She ran toward the main house. Having a woman helping him get the girls to the safe room would be a Godsend for Laird. Finn had a wild hope that the man would push Angie in at the last moment and lock the door.

The sniper rifle had been placed in the guard tower earlier, which was where Drake was currently headed.

As he opened the gun box, he could hear the helicopter coming over the fence. Mason appeared by his side holding one of the assault rifles and handing Finn another. The rotors from the helicopter were kicking up a storm as they landed in the middle of the compound, the sound was loud, but the distinctive sounds of a rifle report were still heard. Drake had found some targets!

"Give us Dasha," came over a loudspeaker.

Finn and Mason went low behind one of the two Hummers. Finn heard a crash, and peeked under the vehicle and saw the first oversized truck crash through the compound's gate, with another one on its heels.

"Wait for it," Mason said with a feral grin on his face.

As the first truck moved closer toward the helicopter on the dirt road, there was a massive explosion, and the truck flew into the air and landed on its side. It was a smoldering wreck. The other truck barely managed to swerve past it. Men were now getting out of the helicopter.

Finn and Mason took aim and hit their targets. There was a barrage of bullets coming back at them.

"They're aiming for the gas tank," Finn growled as he grabbed Mason's arm. Then there were bullets flying past them from the house.

"Get into the house boys." It was Lou! Finn glanced behind him and saw the muzzle of guns from various windows in the house, and realized they had cover to get into the house, or better yet, into the detached garage. That would allow them two angles to fire at the intruders. He pointed, and Mason nodded, then they ran.

"If you get hurt, I'm going to fucking kill you, Gault," he yelled to his commander. With those words, Mason kicked it up a little bit and took the lead. They ended up crashing through the door of the garage at the same time.

Finn slammed the door shut, and Mason went to one of the three windows and smashed it open with the butt of his rifle. He took aim and fired.

"Did you hit something?"

"Nope," Mason said, as he fired again. "But they stopped advancing. Drake hit another one. We have at least four dead out there, not counting the men dead in that truck Laird got with the landmine."

A bullet pinged through one of the other windows.

"Dammit!" Mason took aim again as Finn went to the third window and busted it open and fired.

"Give us Dasha or you will all die." An explosion rocked the garage. Finn and Mason looked at one another. From the angle of the windows, they couldn't see what had happened. Finn went to the back wall of the garage and shot a hole through it, then he could see the cabin that he and Angie had shared was now a burning shell. He took an old filing cabinet and shoved it in front of the hole he had just made and came back to Mason.

"They just blew up one of the cabins."

Mason's cell phone vibrated. He told Finn that it was Drake. "He figures there are six remaining targets. Unfortunately, the way the house and garage were built, it blocks part of his sight."

"This sure sucks as a compound," Finn muttered.

"He did take out the motor on the helicopter."

"Give us Dasha!" the man was screaming now.

"Can't he take out the guy on the microphone?" Finn complained. Mason gave him a weary smile.

"He heard you. He said to tell you he's trying." Mason hung up the phone. They went back to their windows to see if they could get a shot. Finn worried about Angie. Was she shooting? Was she okay? Please God, say she was in the safe room. But deep in his heart, he knew she wasn't.

LAIRD HAD ASSAULT RIFLES TOO, so Angie didn't have to just shoot with her pistol. Sergei was sitting against a far inside wall. He looked gray. Pops didn't look much better. She was upstairs with the two of them, while Laird handled downstairs. When she last saw him, he had looked scarily eager. By the time she'd gotten to the main house, Laird had the girls safely ensconced in the saferoom. As soon as Drake's first shot was fired, Laird shouted for her to go upstairs with her grandfather. He had a brutal grin on his face.

The few shots she had taken had hurt like a son of a bitch. She was going to find Paul Jackson and stomp on *his* fucking ribs. She saw one man lifting his gun to take aim at the garage. She shot at him, grinning when she saw a spurt of blood fly up.

"That'll teach you to try to shoot at my man."

"Did you say something?" Pops asked tiredly.

"Just talking to myself," she assured him. The muzzle of the rifle was supported entirely by the window sill. He was exhausted.

"Do you need to rest?" she asked.

Pops jerked the butt of the rifle to his shoulder and squinted down the barrel. "I'm doing just fine."

A bullet crashed through the window, spraying glass like shrapnel all over her grandfather. She watched in horror as pieces lodged into his cheek, his shoulder, and his hand.

"Lou!" Sergei called out and ran over. Angie looked out and took aim. She could actually see the man grinning at her. She shot the smile off his face. She set the rifle down and lurched over to her granddad's side. He was bleeding a lot.

"Angie, go back to your post," Sergei said. She looked at the man. He was competently dealing with her grandfather's injuries. "Angie, go back to your post," he commanded. She forced herself to stop looking at Pops' injuries and instead looked into the decisive blue eyes of the former Marine sergeant. She nodded.

"Report!" Laird shouted from the first floor.

"We're good!" Sergei shouted. He motioned for her to get moving. She took one last look at her grandfather and went back to the window and picked up her rifle. She glanced over to the right and saw the three little windows in the garage. She smiled grimly as she saw a flash as a bullet was fired out of one of the windows. Angie's gaze was pulled back to the left as she heard the navy blue truck start up.

What the hell?

It started to move. It reminded her of one of the monster trucks she had seen on TV, and it was picking up speed. It was heading towards the front of the house. It couldn't possibly climb the porch stairs, could it?

Angie watched in horror as it ran over two corpses, and slammed up the steps. She felt the reverberations at the same time as she heard the crash of the timber. Oh God, let Laird be okay. She knew the safe room was in the basement and encased by steel, so the girls were safe, but Laird could be injured or dead.

"Angie, move away from the window." She knew that. What was she thinking? She moved and helped Sergei pull her grandfather to the far side of the bedroom, away from the front wall. She heard yelling downstairs and then shots fired. She grabbed her pistol and started towards the door of the room. Sergei grabbed her arm.

"Stay here where it's safe." She threw off his hand.

"Stay with Pops." She left the room, and peered over the railing and saw the shattered living room where the truck had come careening through the space. There was a man hanging out of the passenger seat, he looked dead.

Laird had his knife to the neck of another man. She watched in satisfaction as he plunged it deep. Then she saw a third man crawling out of the cab of the truck, he held up a gun, and she squeezed off a shot. It went wild. Laird turned and ducked. He threw his knife at the man, and it hit his shoulder. Laird ran after his knife, and moments after the knife landed, he tackled him. Angie rushed down the stairs. By the time she got there, Laird was holding the man in a chokehold.

"I'm going to make this motherfucker talk," Laird said through gritted teeth.

Finn pushed his way through the rubble with a man in tow. "Nope, it's going to be this asshole."

Hysterical laughter threatened, but Angie managed to tamp it down. "Who gives a shit which man talks first? Where's Mason? Where's Drake?"

"Mason's calling in the reinforcements," Finn said as he handed off his prisoner to Laird and headed towards her. "Are you okay, baby?"

"We need an ambulance for Pops. Are you sure we got everybody? Where's the general?"

Laird spoke up. "He's not here. According to this asshole, he's waiting for a report. He never left Austin."

Finn took her hand. "Take me to Lou."

She led him upstairs. Sergei had removed the glass, and was in the process of using sheets as bandages."

"I'm okay, Angela," he breathed out, as she rushed to grab his hand.

"Don't ever scare me like that again," she commanded. His brown eyes started to close.

"No, stay awake!"

"Not goin' anywhere. Tired." His hand went lax. She pressed her fingers against his neck, shuddering with relief when she felt his pulse.

"It's okay. He's just unconscious," Sergei explained.

"Where's the ambulance?" Angie cried.

"It'll be faster for Drake to drive you and your grandfather to the hospital in Lake Texoma. We still have a little more cleanup to do before the authorities can be called in," Finn explained.

She looked at him. "What are you going to do?"

"We're going to finish this, Angie." Finn's thumb brushed her cheekbone.

"How?"

"Trust me. You need to be with your grandfather. Trust me to take care of this, okay?" She looked at the man who had been through hell, and tears welled.

"I'll always trust you."

"Drake!" Finn shouted for his friend.

"Right here." Angie turned and saw the large man coming into the room with Laird. They actually had a stretcher.

Laird knelt down beside Pops. "Let me take a look at him." He had a medical kit, and took her grandfather's blood pressure and listened to his heart with a stethoscope. "Angie, he's strong as an ox." He gave Pops a slight shake. "Mr. Donatelli, can you hear me?"

"What?" came the thin response.

"This is Laird. We're going to get you to a hospital."

"Where's Angela?"

"I'm right here, Pops."

"Love you," he slurred, then his eyes closed again.

"He's doing good. I promise," Laird said looking up at

her. He motioned to Drake. "Let's load him up. You're going to the hospital with Angie and Mr. Donatelli."

"I'll go," Sergei said.

"Not you Sergei," Finn said. He had a plan.

THE MEN WATCHED as Sergei wielded the knife right below the man's eye. He was speaking in Ukrainian. A pinprick of blood welled beneath the man's eye socket.

Sergei took the knife away, and started to clean his nails with it since it was Finn's huge K-Bar, he knew just how much skill and delicacy was required. The man knew his way around knives, and it was scaring the piss out of the Ukrainian soldier. Everything in Finn's soul approved.

"He said he is a Special Forces soldier and will not tell us anything." Sergei laughed.

The soldier was tied tightly to the chair in what was left of Laird's office. The old marine sliced a long line along the soldier's upturned palm with the K-Bar. He screamed. Finn looked on with fascination. The cut exactly mirrored the man's lifeline.

Fuck, Sergei was good with knives.

The old man crouched in front of the prisoner and yelled in his face, spittle hitting him. The man cringed. He kept trying to respond, but Sergei talked over him until finally he stopped and let him speak. The soldier was obviously begging.

"He said that when he returns, he will tell the general Dasha died in the attack." Sergei laughed. "Close, but no cigar."

Sergei gave the man a gentle smile and cupped his cheek. He said something softly in their native language.

The man frantically shook his head no. Again he was begging. The old marine persisted. The man started to cry, continuing to shake his head.

Sergei turned and looked at the other men in the room. "He doesn't want to tell us where his general is." Finn shivered, but not with shock, or revulsion. No something dark and ugly reared its head. It delighted in what he was sure was going to come next.

Sergei turned and smiled broadly at the soldier and said something in Ukrainian, then started cutting off the man's pants. For an instant, the room changed, and he was once more in Canada with his gun shoved in Albert Liu's crotch, revenge roaring through his blood.

When Sergei exposed the soldier's penis, he pressed the knife beneath the tip, and the soldier started babbling. The man was crying as the blood dripped down from the cut under his eye and his hand.

"Ahh, we have a location. He is in Austin. What a popular town."

"Now you will call your leader, and tell him you have the girl and are bringing her to him. Do you understand?" The man nodded. Defeated.

They gave the man the cell phone they had confiscated. "Call the general," Sergei demanded. "If you say one thing wrong, I will not kill you. I will castrate you."

Finn watched and listened as he made his call. The general was going to meet them at Lou's ranch. As soon as it ended, he dropped the phone and started crying. Sergei laughed. He turned to Finn.

"It is done."

What did he mean it was done?

It wasn't even *close* to being done. Why hadn't he killed the man? Finn took two steps forward toward Sergei, intent on taking his knife out of the old Marine's hand. If Sergei wouldn't finish the job than Finn sure as fuck would.

Stop! Breathe!

He took a deep breath and looked away from the knife in Sergei's hand. He took another look at the man in the chair. He was sobbing. Was it done? Maybe it was. He took another deep breath and turned away. He saw Mason looking at him, assessing.

"YOU NEED ME. I speak his language," Sergei insisted. Finn wasn't sure which language the old Ukrainian man was referring to—their native tongue or the brutality. But then again, who was he to talk? He had enjoyed every fucking minute of Sergei's questioning of the soldier.

"Sergei, Mason and I have this. You need to stay with the girls. Laird will have his hands full without you." Sergei gave him a hard look.

"This man is an animal. You must not be afraid to put him down." Sergei's gnarled hands clenched into fists.

"We will make sure he is no longer a threat to your niece," Mason assured him. Sergei dismissed Mason and looked long and hard at Finn as if he saw a kindred spirit.

"Mason is right. Dasha will no longer have anything to fear."

"Don't underestimate the man, even with the call, he'll be on alert for trouble. Once he sees you don't have Dasha, he will shoot to kill," Sergei warned.

"We know," Finn assured him. "Everything we've discussed makes our plan perfect. We can ambush him. You know this will work."

"But I've lived on the ranch for the last six weeks, I'll be an asset."

"Sergei, you'll have to trust us." Mason's tone brooked no argument.

"Yes, sir," Sergei acquiesced.

They trudged out to Drake's rental truck that miraculously had only suffered minor damage during the shootout.

"Do you think anybody will notice a few bullet holes?" Mason asked.

"Nah, it's Texas. Well, Oklahoma," Finn qualified. "But soon to be Texas. We'll be fine."

"I'll drive first, you can rest. Then we'll switch," Mason said.

"I'm too keyed up to sleep," Finn said.

"Then rest your eyes. You need some shut-eye." Mason's tone was softer than with Sergei, but he still expected Finn to obey him. The thing was, Finn knew Mason only did it for his own good.

Finn climbed into the passenger seat and was amazed at how fast he fell asleep. He jerked awake when some kind of nightmare caught him sideways. Somebody had been holding Angie one handed, over a cliff. They threw her over, and he hadn't been able to catch her. He was dripping wet with sweat.

Mason was partly looking at the road, and partly looking over at him. "You okay, Finn?"

"Fine," he clipped out his answer fast, not wanting to talk about it.

"Want to drive?"

"Sure." Happy at the idea of something to take his mind off of the nightmare.

They had to go a couple of miles more down the freeway before there was a place to pull over.

"You sure you're good?" Mason's voice was even, but it still rubbed Finn the wrong way.

"I said yes, already," Finn snapped. Mason just nodded and got out of the driver's side, and they switched seats. God, his head hurt. He didn't have any sunglasses. He felt like a piece of shit for the way he had talked to Mase. He just continued to fuck up all over the place.

"When do you think we're going to hear from Drake?" Finn asked.

"He called while you were asleep. He's about two hours behind us. He'll meet us at your apartment." Finn gripped the steering wheel tightly.

"Don't trust me, huh?" As soon as the words were out of his mouth, he regretted them. Mason stayed silent. "Can I get a do-over?"

"God, Finn. I would prefer it if we could do over a lot," Mason said quietly. "You're really afraid I don't trust you?"

"How can you, Mase? I don't fucking trust myself." Finn could taste the bitterness coating his tongue.

"You're one of my men. You've saved my life. You've literally, all bullshit aside, saved my life, three fucking times Finn." The steering wheel was slippery, and his head pounded.

"That was before," he whispered.

"You're the same man. You're Finn *Fucking* Crandall." Finn could hear Mason's furious attempt to get through to him, but it was like the words were coming from the end of a long tunnel.

"I was."

"You are!" Mason said passionately. "I know you have issues. Fuck, we all have them. But it hasn't changed the man you are. You're always going to be Finn. You're always going to be a man I admire, respect, and love. Are you hearing me?"

"Fine. I am. I'm getting there. But then, like tonight, I'm not there. I'm back. Do you know how badly I wanted to pick up that knife and chop off that guy's dick? I have this sickness that crawls inside of my head. And that's not the worst of it." He stopped talking. Just stared at the road. Watched, as miles crept by.

Finally, Mason asked, "What's the worst?"

"For just a minute tonight, I wasn't in the present. I thought I was in another room. I literally thought I was somewhere else. My head still isn't right Mason." He gulped the bile back and had to swallow the sick taste.

"That's part of it," Mason said calmly. Just hearing him say it like that helped. "I know you. You've researched this to death. You know this part of the illness."

"I do. Why do you think I took leave? I thought with time and distance I could heal."

"Then you decided to get right back into the thick of things." Mason sighed.

"Well, I didn't think it was going to be like this. I thought I was just going to search for Dasha's baby, which I've failed to find," Finn said tiredly.

"Rylie and Lydia should have a name soon, now that they've tracked her to Indianapolis. You know this."

"And I've done nothing."

Mason laughed. "Beat yourself up much, Crandall?"

That stopped him. "Uhm, maybe?"

"Uhm, a lot." They both laughed. "Let me help you put this into perspective. You've helped to save Dasha's life, and the lives of all the other girls from this fucking Ukrainian monster." Mason took a deep breath. "But that's the heart of the matter, you can't see anything good that you've done. Can you?"

"No, I guess I can't. I only seem to focus on my failures."

Finn paused. "That's not totally true. Angie helps me see the positives."

Mason laughed. It was a long laugh. Finn turned his head from the highway to look at him. "What?"

"I think you've just found one of the secrets."

"What do you mean?"

"Sophia was a Godsend when I was having trouble losing Larry back on that mission three years ago." Finn remembered how closed off Mason had been after that. They had all worried about him.

"Angie brings light into my life."

"Same with Sophia." Finn wondered if he said Angie's name the same way Mason said Sophia's name.

"But I can't depend on her for that. That's not fair to her. I think. I think..." he stuttered to a stop.

Mason didn't say anything, he just waited patiently.

"I need help. I need counseling."

"Finn, you know there is no stigma attached to that, don't you?"

"You should have accepted my resignation."

"Not a chance in hell."

"You're going to have to put me as *sick in quarters*."

"I'll just have you reassigned for a while." Finn felt a weight lift. He hadn't wanted that. He wanted to be useful. He wanted to continue to contribute to the team. But he hadn't wanted to be a liability.

"What would I do?"

"You'd still support us, just stateside. Let me handle it. In the meantime, since we've talked through all the hard stuff. Can we please get some food and hash out the plan? Drake isn't due for two more hours."

Finn thought about waiting for Drake, but figured they

could get an order to go. He was just happy they had hashed out the touchy-feely shit.

"I know just the place." Finn grinned.

As THEY PULLED into Finn's apartment parking lot, they saw two figures waiting by Finn's El Camino.

"God damn it!" Finn said as he saw Angie.

As soon as the truck stopped, he jumped out and ran over to her and Drake.

"Goddammit, Avery. What the fuck were you thinking?" He shoved Drake, and he slammed into the side of the El Camino. He dented the car, and he couldn't care less.

"I have a plan," Drake said. "Angie knows her granddad's ranch like the back of her hand, so this is perfect."

"I don't want to listen to one of your hair brained plans," Finn yelled.

"We're going to listen to the plan, and then we're sending Angie back to the hospital," Mason said reasonably. That calmed Finn down.

"Finn, don't you dare act like I'm not here," Angie said in a quiet and savage tone.

Ooops.

"Angie's a sharpshooter. We have her go up on the ridge. This part is her idea, we ride horses from a neighbor's ranch to get to the back side of the ridge in case the general is already there, which we know he already could be."

Mason turned to Drake and Angie. "That's a great addition to what we already have. You'd have to wait until they make a move on us. Otherwise, it's murder. They will end up drawing their guns. We'll make sure they draw on us. As soon as that happens, you go for it."

"It's Angie Oakley and me." Drake grinned.

"Look you, big oaf, I said not to call me that." Angie backhanded him in his stomach.

ANGIE LOOKED at the burnt shell of her grandfather's ranch, the decimation confronting her took her breath away. She worked hard to quell her tears of heartbreak and rage. Drake must have read her.

"Damn, Angie, I'm so sorry." She was surprised how caring Drake sounded.

"It's all right." Blowing off his sympathy.

"No, it's not. We're going to get those bastards." Through their rifles, they were able to see five men hidden around the property, and what looked like two more in a car. She and Drake watched as the black truck drove up the drive. Finn and Mason got out and closed the doors, miming to someone in the backseat. It looked believable that Dasha was there.

The plan was for Mason and Finn to ask the general what information Dasha had, that she could give him. And then they would take her back. That was the reason for the talk, to begin with. The two men got out of the car, one clearly in charge. He moved forward and starting yelling at Mason and Finn. They could hear the voice but not the words.

"I wish I knew what the asshat was saying," Drake said.

"I wish I could take a shot," Angie murmured. She had her sights set on the man's head.

They heard Mason speaking, his voice carried, but not the words. She sighed in frustration. The general tried to push past him. Both Finn and Mason pushed him back. The second man joined the fray and pulled a gun. Finn easily hit it out of his hands and pointed it at the man. The general yelled. A flash and the sound of a shot rang out.

Drake shot.

"Got the shooter."

"Fuck, can't get the general, he's too close to Mason," Angie said.

"Finn will get the fucker." Drake shot again, as more shots were made down at the ranch. Angie changed her sights, looking and finding one of the other men she had scoped out earlier. She took the shot and killed him. She heard Drake take another shot. That should be two that he had gotten. She veered back to the general and the second man. Finn had the general on the ground, she saw with satisfaction. The other man was dead.

"FINN. NO!" a voice yelled out. The voice came from a long way off.

Finn had his knife shoved against the general's throat. Was that Mason? He saw blood trickling beneath his knife, and the whites of the general's eyes were clearly visible. It made him happy. A hand clamped down on his shoulder. He shoved it away.

"Please no," the general begged.

"You are such a pussy. Do you understand that word?" Finn purred.

"Yes," he croaked out.

"Nod." Finn pressed the knife tip under the man's chin.

"Yes, I understand. I am a pussy."

"Nod, you motherfucker," Finn ground out.

Slowly he nodded. Finn watched in satisfaction as the

knife cut into his chin, and a line of blood welled up and started to drip down his throat.

"Finn, you need to stop," a voice said softly into his ear. *Why was somebody whispering in his ear? Was the voice even real? It sounded familiar.*

He looked down and smiled. The blood looked pretty.

"Nod again."

He smelled urine. Another thing that made him happy.

A brotherly hand rested on his shoulder. "Finn, can you hear me? It's Mason."

Mason was here? He looked down and saw blood on the man's chin. Vlad. His name was Vlad. He pulled back his knife.

"Give me the knife." A hand appeared in front of his eyes. He looked to his right, and Mason was crouched beside him. He smiled reassuringly.

"What?" Finn asked.

"Finn, can you give me the knife, buddy?"

"I need it. I have to kill this guy. He's bad."

"I'll take care of him, okay? You trust me, don't you?" Mason squeezed his shoulder.

Finn gave him a considering look and smiled. "Yeah, I trust you. Here." He handed Mason the knife.

Why was there blood on it?

Oh, Fuck. Not again.

"You saved me," Mason said quietly as they took the general to the back of the truck.

He knew Mason had been talking for about twenty minutes. But it was all bullshit. He needed to get away.

238 | CAITLYN O'LEARY

Quick. Maybe he could take the car the general had arrived in.

The zip ties secured Vlad's wrists and ankles as they threw him in the back. Then Mason shoved Finn against the hood of the car.

"Can you hear me, Crandall?"

"What?" Finn shook his head. "He had his gun pointed to my heart, and you pulled the gun away. First, it was pointed at you, and you turned it so it shot his sidekick. You risked your life to save mine—again." Finn saw the savage sincerity in Mason's eyes. He wasn't kidding.

"What are you talking about?" All Finn remembered was having the general under his knife. He remembered the general practically spitting as he demanded Dasha.

"Angie and Drake will back me up."

"Then what happened?"

"You got out your knife and went a Sergei on the bastard."

Finn sighed. He heard the rumble of horses.

"Finn!" Angie cried out. He turned and saw Angie Oakley sliding off her horse and running towards him. "You scared the piss out of me." She'd seen his freak out.

"I know."

"When you went to knock that gun away, I thought you were going to die. Don't do that again." She pounded his chest. Then she winced. Dammit, she shouldn't have been riding a horse. Her rib still wasn't mended.

"We need to get you to the doctor."

"Nice save, Crandall," Drake said as he pounded Finn's back. "I like working for Mason, wouldn't want to have to break-in a new lieutenant."

"What are you two talking about? I was about ready to cut the general to ribbons?"

"So?" Drake said.

Finn huffed out a laugh. His friend was a little bloodthirsty.

"I don't remember much. I was having an episode."

"So get into therapy," Drake said easily. "All that matters is you saved Mason. Concentrate on the important shit, man."

Mason looked at him. "I told you, you fucking saved me. This is now number four. This is the fourth fucking time you saved my life. You're Finn *Fucking* Crandall. You're a hero."

"He's my hero," Angie said, reaching up and kissing him. Finn felt his heart swell. He would be able to make it through this. He had the right people surrounding him. He was Finn Fucking Crandall.

EPILOGUE

One Month Later...

Finn had never held a baby before in his life.

"You should be holding her," he whispered.

"You're doing great," Angie said for the forty-seventh time. Finn saw the door up ahead. Dasha was on the other side. They hadn't told her Yulia was coming home, in case something went wrong. They didn't want to get her hopes up. They walked up the steps of the Preston Ranch.

Before they could even knock, Richard Preston opened the door. His eyes lit up.

"There's our girl. She's beautiful." His large finger brushed Yulia's cheek. Finn was amazed at how at ease the man was with the baby. "Dasha's in the great room with my wife and Penelope. Let's go."

Angie and Finn followed him. They were in the room concentrating on something on the coffee table. They looked up as Angie and Finn entered the room, and Dasha cried out. She went to stand up, but Grace and Penelope each held an arm, holding her to the couch.

Finn walked over and knelt in front of her.

"My Yulia?" Dasha looked at Finn for confirmation. Then looking down at the healthy baby who was thrashing and smiling in her pink blanket, Dasha reached out with a trembling hand and touched Yulia's lips.

"Baby." She sighed. Then she started talking in Ukrainian. The girl had tears falling down her face. Her hands were trembling so badly, Grace helped her sit back, and Finn placed Yulia in her arms.

Dasha pressed her face next to her daughter's and breathed in. All the while talking in her native language.

"She says welcome home, my love. I have prayed every day for you. You are my heart. My soul. You mean everything to me," Sergei translated as he stood behind the sofa.

Finn felt tears on his cheeks. Angie was also crying. He took her hand. Sergei came around the couch.

"Thank you both so much for everything," the old man said.

"You're welcome." Finn shook his hand, and Angie hugged him and kissed his cheek. "Dasha remembering which bank of lockers really helped. They just opened them all. They got the evidence they needed."

"Really? Thank God. Dasha's been so worried." Sergei looked to where Dasha cuddled her baby and smiled.

"Tell her she has nothing to worry about. He's going back to the Ukraine, where he will pay for his crimes. Dasha is a hero," Finn said.

Sergei beamed.

Grace got off the couch and came up to them.

"I have a room made up for you. I know you came straight from Indianapolis. Dinner will be in two hours."

"We really should be going," Angie protested.

"Nonsense. Rosa will show you the way. I would, but..." She pointed towards her cane and laughed.

"Come with me," Rosa said with a smile. "We are having a celebration dinner. You are our guests of honor. I have baked a cake. You are spending the night." Angie grabbed Finn's hand and squeezed when he would have protested about spending the night. As soon as they were settled in their room, he turned to her.

"Why are you letting them bulldoze us into staying? I thought you wanted to go home tonight."

"It's called southern hospitality. We stay." She looked at him intently. "Plus, you're tired." He felt something melt inside him, as she once again cared for him.

"I love you, Angie," he said as he pulled her into his arms. "Can we make use of the bed?"

"That's why they sent us to nap," she said using air quotes around the word nap.

"Can you sit down for a moment? I want to talk to you about the last month I spent in San Diego." He watched as she trembled.

Dammit.

"There's more than what you've told me on the phone and Skype?" she asked hesitantly.

"I've realized just how slow of a process this is going to be. I thought after a month, I would be closer to being cured. This could take months, maybe even a year or more, before I'm team ready."

Angie cupped his face and placed a gentle kiss on his lips. "You know that's okay, don't you?"

"No, I really don't. But we're working on that too." He

hugged her closer. "I feel like my whole life is on hold. Or should be. You know?"

Her face was unreadable. She nodded. "You need to do what you think is best."

"But here's the thing. What Dasha said is the truth. You're my heart. You're my soul. Every day we're away from one another, rips me apart."

It was like sunlight burst across her face. "I feel the same way."

"I still think I'm a bad bet," he said against her lips.

"You're a royal flush, and I claimed you."

"I'm claiming you back. Marry me. I don't know how our careers will work, where we'll live. But I need to be with you. Please just marry me."

"I want to sleep beside you every night," she said as she kissed him back. "Moving forward with you every day is the most important thing."

"Now I can finally look forward to my future."

ABOUT THE AUTHOR

Caitlyn O'Leary is an avid reader and considers herself a fan first and an author second. She reads a wide variety of genres but finds herself going back to happily-ever-afters. Getting a chance to write, after years in corporate America, is a dream come true. She hopes her stories provide the kind of entertainment and escape she has found from some of her favorite authors.

As of winter 2018 she has fourteen books in her two best-selling Navy SEAL series; Midnight Delta and Black Dawn. What makes them special is their bond to one another, and the women they come to love.

She also writes a Paranormal series called the Found. It's been called a Military / Sci-Fi / Action-Adventure thrill ride. The characters have special abilities, that make them targets.

The books that launched her career, is a steamy and loving menage series called Fate Harbor. It focuses on a tight knit community in Fate Harbor Washington, who live, love and care for one another.

Her other two series are The Sisters and the Shadow Alliance. You will be seeing more for these series in 2018.

Keep up with Caitlyn O'Leary:

Facebook: tinyurl.com/nuhvey2
Twitter: @CaitlynOLearyNA
Pinterest: tinyurl.com/q36uohc
Goodreads: tinyurl.com/nqy66h7
Website: www.caitlynoleary.com
Email: caitlyn@caitlynoleary.com
Newsletter: http://bit.ly/1WIhRup
Instagram: http://bit.ly/29WaNIh

ALSO BY CAITLYN O'LEARY

Made in United States
Orlando, FL
27 December 2021

12578824R00143